T0198634

IN COMMON

SANDRA COOPER

BALBOA.
PRESS
A DIVISION OF HAY HOUSE

Balboa Press books may be ordered through booksellers or by contacting:

Balboa Press
A Division of Hay House
1663 Liberty Drive
Bloomington, IN 47403
www.balboapress.com
1 (877) 407-4847

Because of the dynamic nature of the Internet, any web addresses or links contained in this book may have changed since publication and may no longer be valid. The views expressed in this work are solely those of the author and do not necessarily reflect the views of the publisher, and the publisher hereby disclaims any responsibility for them.

The author of this book does not dispense medical advice or prescribe the use of any technique as a form of treatment for physical, emotional, or medical problems without the advice of a physician, either directly or indirectly. The intent of the author is only to offer information of a general nature to help you in your quest for emotional and spiritual well-being. In the event you use any of the information in this book for yourself, which is your constitutional right, the author and the publisher assume no responsibility for your actions.

Any people depicted in stock imagery provided by Thinkstock are models, and such images are being used for illustrative purposes only. Certain stock imagery © Thinkstock.

Print information available on the last page.

ISBN: 978-1-5043-3514-0 (sc)
ISBN: 978-1-5043-3515-7 (hc)
ISBN: 978-1-5043-3516-4 (e)

Library of Congress Control Number: 2015909776

Balboa Press rev. date: 06/17/2015

CONTENTS

Preface vii
Dedication ix
Acknowledgments xi

Chapter 1 They Should Have Named Me Danger 1
Chapter 2 Becoming Just Another House Nigger 7
Chapter 3 Just Sweet Music 13
Chapter 4 Rumor/Truth 19
Chapter 5 Strawberries 25
Chapter 6 Wanting to Hate Miss Sister 29
Chapter 7 Lost Identity 33
Chapter 8 Shameful for a Woman to Discuss 37
Chapter 9 My Parents' Hearts Revealed 43
Chapter 10 Horrors of Life Spill Out 53
Chapter 11 Bitterness/Sweetness 61
Chapter 12 Making Things Right 67
Chapter 13 Two Mothers 71
Chapter 14 Little Andy Becomes Andrew 83
Chapter 15 Peace Finds Us 93
Chapter 16 Justly So 99

PREFACE

In Common is the life story of Margaret Jefferson-Butler, an old Southern belle born on her family's slave plantation in Florida during the 1800s. The journey unfolds as Margaret sits on the porch talking to her dog, Someday. While sipping on a cool glass of lemonade, she shares the details of her life and its deep-rooted pain. The story continues as Margaret tells of how their relationship was the only thing that gave Miss Sister and her strength to endure a life full of grief caused by the evilness of the white man's way of living.

In the end, the reader gets to see Margaret up close and hear her pain as she realizes how much the white woman and black woman have in common and gets the revelation that the white man believes that he is their master.

DEDICATION

In Common is a story that touches on the plight of women, whether white or black, and the men in our society who think it is their appointed duty to exercise control over our lives. So I dedicate this book to women of the Deep South, and to women the world over who have experienced the oppression of male domination and control but dared to speak out.

ACKNOWLEDGMENTS

Blessings! That is what I have received in writing this book. My faith in an all-supreme God has gotten me through the rough times, the times when the thoughts did not flow, and the times when I wanted to give up.

Carol Carr, with whom I first shared my idea for *In Common*, provided the enthusiasm and excitement that gave me the courage to write this heartfelt story.

My son Belvin McClinton II kept me focused and sacrificed much of his time for the success of this story. Belvin has been a tremendous blessing; he respected my writing time and the solitude that writing requires.

My son Muzik McClinton and my daughter-in-law, Kimonicia, were an endless source of love and encouragement.

My granddaughters, ConSandra and Conmina McClinton, merit mention, for they are the future generation, as do all of my other family members and friends who supported me during this journey. My editors and those who gave me guidance have been blessings to me.

Finally, I would like to thank Lisa Hendricks, Fulton County Georgia Advocate of the Victim Witness Program. Lisa is God's angel who labored faithfully with me as I went through the process of being healed from the pain of domestic violence.

1

THEY SHOULD HAVE NAMED ME DANGER

It was a hot, sunny day around the year 1820 in the deep south of Florida, on the forever-reaching acres of the Butler Plantation. There, far back from the road, surrounded by many trees, was the big house in all of its splendor—a white, prestigious mansion with a weeping willow on the left side and a lemon tree on the right. The mansion was so hidden behind an assortment of beautiful flowers and hedges that it appeared to be growing right out of the shrubbery. That was where I, Margaret Butler, an old southern belle, sat on the big wraparound porch, drinking a cool glass of lemonade with Someday, my dog.

You know, there was only one person who understood my pain, shared my relief, and safeguarded the secrets of my heart—only one whom I trusted more than my child, more than my mama and papa, and, if I had a brother, more than him, too. That person was Miss Sister. Why, Miss Sister was the name I gave her when I was just a little girl. I was an only child, and my cousins and best friends had sisters. I wanted one, too. So as Miss Sister called me Miss Margaret, I decided to call her Miss Sister, and that was that. My mama tried hard to change my mind, but even as a child I was stubborn, and I set out not to have it any other way.

Why, I remember one day, when I was about five years old, Papa had allowed Miss Sister to go into town with us, and while we were in the store, a man heard me calling her Miss Sister.

He asked, "Girl, why you calling that nigger gal 'miss'?"

I replied, "'Cause I want to."

Well, he turned redder that a red bird and almost choked on his chewing tobacco as he was rushing out that store. I guess it took him by surprise that a five-year-old thought like that. So eventually everybody came to know her as Miss Sister. Miss Sister was the only name I knew until much later, when I learned her given name was Violet—but still I preferred Miss Sister. Miss Sister fully understood me, and I, in turn, knew her just as well.

I rubbed Someday down his back and began to daydream about our childhood days.

As far back as I could remember, there was a Miss Sister. Her family was owned by my father, and her mama was my mother's lady's maid. Since I had no brothers or sisters, Mama would allow me to bring Miss Sister in the house to keep me company. She was three years older than me, and even as a child, she was taller than the children her own age. Her complexion was a pecan brown, and she had coarse hair that she always wore in two long braids down her back because that was her way of taking control of it. Hell, it was the only thing that she was allowed to control. She had no control over where to live, how to live, or just plain living. But those eyes of hers were so big they demanded everyone's attention. Those eyes shouted, "Don't you dare ignore me!" Those eyes could swallow you up in just one look. But even so, she was the most beautiful slave I had ever seen.

As a child, I was always getting into trouble for trying to figure out why and how something was done—and usually the something was really none of my business. My Uncle Charlie, for instance, was a snuff sniffer and never ceased to amaze me as I watched him putting that brown stuff up his nose, wondering why he did that. Well, my mind led me to believe that it must have been something real good, like sucking on candy. So one particular day, he laid his snuff box down and forgot to close it, and I politely took it and eased away to the porch. It was on a Sunday, and I was still dressed up from church in my beautiful, buttercup-yellow dress. I poured some of the dark powder in my hand and put my nose in it, but that didn't work. All I did was smear the stuff on my nose and top lip while the rest of it landed on my dress. Still determined to get it up my nose, I then decided to lie down on the porch, roll over, and put more in my hand to try to get it in my nose while I held my head back, but then it ended up in my eyes. Why, my mama said she had never heard such screaming and crying in all her life. After that, my uncle Charlie would always poke fun at me by inviting me to take some snuff with him. But my snuff-sniffing days were done.

Trust. I learned to trust Miss Sister way back when I was a child. Really, I owed her my life. When I was about fifteen years old, I remember one day, Rebecca, Jenney, my cousin Betty Jean, and I overheard Calvin and Josh planning to meet at the lake that evening to go skinny-dipping. So I talked the girls into slipping out the house to meet down there and surprise them by showing up at the lake as well. When we got there, it was dark, and the boys were already in the water.

"What y'all girls doin' here?" Calvin yelled.

Without a moment of hesitation, I answered, "I think we are here for the same reason y'all is—and besides, Calvin, who died and made you my papa?"

Calvin just gave me that dumb, blank look that only he could give. I was taking off my clothes when I realized that the other girls were just standing and staring.

"Well, now, don't tell me I got a bunch of scared-asses hangin' around me. I thought y'all came to get in the water." I enjoyed daring them in front of the boys. Finally they followed my lead.

The weather was so hot that night, but we were excited—the boys were there with us, and we were taking a chance on getting caught. Lord, I reckon Mama would have nearly died if she had known that her daughter was doing the forbidden things of life. I lived for danger. Just hearing I could not do something gave me a reason to prove that I could—and I would, in spite of what anybody else thought. I was quite a daredevil. But on that night, after my final jump in the water, all I remember after that was Miss Sister bent over me, calling my name while the others cried. I had almost drowned, but Miss Sister came from out of nowhere like God's angel and saved me. The others had panicked, and this could have cost me my life. Not only did she save me from that, but she also saved me from the wrath of Mama and Papa.

I could still see her helping me to sneak back into the house and safely into bed and hear her saying, "Why, Miss Margaret, when I saw you headed that way, I could smell trouble on hand. Figured I'd best follow you. Lord knows that I am glad I did. Now, don't you go worryin' none, Miss Margaret. I won't tell a soul. You just rest easy now. This matter is safe with me. Why, Miss Margaret, I swear my lips will not part to tell anybody what you got yourself into this night."

That night she slept on the floor beside my bed, making sure I was all right. She risked her life for me. One day, I realized the truth of the matter was that if I had drowned, everyone would have blamed her. It did not matter that I placed my own self in harm's way. All they would consider is that a slave had failed at saving a white girl. I had many nightmares of that incident, but still that did not stop me from going back to the lake. Every time they dared me, I went.

Now there was another time when Miss Sister and I were picking blackberries down in the woods and I almost got bit by a snake, but Miss Sister was right there chopping his head off. That snake never saw it coming.

I was scared that time, but to help me save face, Miss Sister built a fire, cooked that snake right there in the woods, and told me, "Miss Margaret, eat a piece, and gain power over this here devil." Then Miss Sister started jumping round doing some kind of buck dance while I ate a piece of that snake. And just as she said, when I swallowed it down, I felt the power rise up in me. Like I said, any time I felt like somebody was daring me to do something, I did it. My mama and papa should have named me Danger.

2

BECOMING JUST ANOTHER HOUSE NIGGER

As I reached for my glass of lemonade, I noticed that Someday had gone to the top of the porch steps as if he'd seen something, but it turned out to be just a bird in the bushes.

"Oh, Someday, there you go chasing things again. Come back here and sit down. It's just a bird."

Sometimes I wonder if God, knowing how foolish I would be, decided to create Miss Sister just to watch out for me. I think that somehow she got pleasure from my misbehaving. I would do whatever and then we would have a high time laughing about it. As far as I was concerned, I had more fun with Miss Sister than I could ever have had with a sister of my own.

That was the way it remained between us until the year that I got married. Papa had promised Simon, the stable boy, that he would allow Simon to jump the broom with Miss Sister. Lord, that girl was so happy—almost happier than I was when Gabriel and I first became engaged. She really loved Simon. Excited, we would sit and contemplate how it would be on our wedding night. We both were still virgins, and even though I never gave a second thought about misbehaving, I never wanted to have intercourse before getting married. This was one thing I was going to do the right way.

We were closer than two peas in a pod—but things changed rapidly for us when, for some reason, Papa changed his mind about Miss Sister and Simon jumping the broom and instead gave Miss Sister to Gabriel as a wedding gift. I could not understand why, and Papa refused to explain. Now she went from being closer than a sister to just being another house nigger. Something died in her, and something rose up in me. It was as if the life had left those big, beautiful eyes and sadness had taken up residence instead. Now she would be separated for life from her beloved Simon because Gabriel and I were moving to the plantation that his granddaddy had left him. I confronted Papa, asking why they could not marry and leave with us, but Papa said he could not part with Simon because he was one of his most valuable workers.

"Then why not give one of the other slaves to Gabriel and let Miss Sister stay here?" I asked, confused. But Papa, being so stubborn, held his ground, and with the raising of his voice, I knew that it was better for me to leave this matter alone.

It was no surprise that Gabriel and I got married—after all, we had grown up together. Me being such a tomboy and all, I would try to outrace him, beat him at horseshoes, and do anything else, even though he was older than me. I did not care—I tried anyway. One day, our families were attending a picnic, and all the town's people were there. We had so much fun. Why, I remember putting a baby frog in his shoe that day while he bathed his feet in the pond, and I thought that I would die from laughing at the way he looked when he realized what I had done. I laughed so hard that I found myself holding on tight to my stomach.

The fun continued throughout our childhood days until he was sent away to boarding school—High Point, to be specific, the most prestigious school in the South for boys. It was family tradition to send the boys away to receive the best education. This was the family's way of preparing them for life. But I did not care.

All I felt was that this was their way of destroying my life. Why, I missed Gabriel so much that I was fighting anybody that looked my way, boys and girls alike.

Some days I could not eat. Miss Sister was the only one who could figure it all out, and when she did, she said, "Why, Miss Margaret, you cuttin' up big time over that boy, Gabriel. Been sourer than sour grapes since he left. You think beatin' everybody up is gonna help? Well, I tell you, it won't. You makin' enemies here, and I bet you he is off makin' friends. You gonna starve yourself to death, Miss Margaret? For what? You already skinner than a polecat. You best to think three times about this matter here. My mama always says if somethin' seems to be hard for me, then all I need to do is think on that thing three times, and then I would come to know just what I needed to know. So I am tellin' you, Miss Margaret, for your own good, you need to think three times on this so you can come to your senses."

Miss Sister kept on talking to me and making me laugh whenever she could until finally it did not hurt, nor did Gabriel cross my mind anymore. When we're children, small things can seem to be bigger than the world itself and much more important.

Years went by, and one day, while Papa and I were in the general store, Judge Paul Butler came in with this tall, handsome young man, and our fathers reintroduced us.

"Good afternoon, Judge Butler, and how are you doin' on this fine day?" Papa asked.

"Why, Andrew Jefferson, I am doin' just fine, thank you." Then he tilted his hat as he acknowledged me. "And you, Miss Margaret?"

"I am doin' well. Thank you for askin', sir," I replied.

"Y'all do remember my son Gabriel?" he asked.

We looked at each other and smiled. Why, I was so surprised and thought I was going to melt like butter when he complimented me as he reached for my hand.

Right there in the general store, he said, "Why, Miss Margaret, I would never have guessed it to be you. You were such a skinny little tomboy, but my, my, how you have grown to be such a beautiful young lady." Right then and there, he captured my heart, and I could only hope that I had done the same to him.

After leaving the store that day, it seemed as if it would take forever for Papa and me to reach home. I could hardly wait to tell Miss Sister about what had happened in the store. Finally, we got there, and I rushed in the house to find Miss Sister helping her mama in the kitchen by peeling potatoes.

Dancing around in excitement, I begged, "Cora, will you please excuse Miss Sister to come upstairs with me? Please, pretty, pretty please, Cora."

She looked at me, her hands on her hips, and proceeded to say, "Now, Miss Margaret, you know that Master Jefferson is goin' to be expectin' for his dinner to be served on time. Child, can't it wait?"

"Cora, it will only take just a moment. You don't want me to die from the anticipation of showin' her somethin' I purchased in the general store, now, do you?"

Cora looked at Miss Sister and, realizing that she was excited about finding out just what it was, said, "All right, but do it quickly and get right back here."

Before Cora could finish getting those words out her mouth, we had ran up the stairs and into my bedroom.

"Guess what happened today, Miss Sister," I said, with a big grin on my face.

"Child, I am not goin' to try to guess," she replied, "but you best to tell me, Miss Margaret, and tell me right now, 'cause I know from the look on your face that it is somethin' I need to hear. Tell me right now or I am goin' to tickle it out of you."

Then she started ticklin' me, and I began to laugh. Finally, when I could take it no more, I shouted, "Okay, okay! I'll tell you.

10

I saw Gabriel Butler in the general store with Judge Butler. He is back! Gabriel is back, Miss Sister!"

"Gabriel Butler—that boy you almost starved to death over? Tell me, how did he look? What did he say? Tell me everything!" she said.

"Well, at first he didn't know who I was. But when he finally recognized me, he reached for my hand and said that I had grown to be such a beautiful young lady. I almost died of disbelief while standin' there lookin' at that tall, blond, blue-eyed angel standin' right before me."

At this time, I was fannin' my face with both my hands. "It was if I had died and gone to heaven, and if Papa had not been there, I would have believed just that."

Before I could say anything else, we were interrupted by Cora calling Miss Sister. "If she asks what I wanted," I said, "it was just to show you this dress I bought."

"Okay," Miss Sister said, "I best to be goin' now before Mama tans my hide. But we'll finish later." She left the room, both of us sure we would be looking forward to completing this conversation at bedtime.

JUST SWEET MUSIC

After a while of just rocking and thinking, I said to Someday, "You bein' just a dog don't have to put up with matters of the heart."

Anyway, months went by, and the only time I saw Gabriel was on Sundays at church. He would just speak to me and continue on his way. My young heart was tortured because deep inside of me, I still had those endearing feelings for him. But right when I felt that there was no hope in this cause, one afternoon Papa returned from purchasing horses with this strange look on his face.

He placed his arm around my shoulder and said, "Margaret, guess who I saw today?"

I looked at him with no clue who he was talking about. "Who, Papa? Tell me—who did you see?" I asked.

"I saw Judge Butler and his son Gabriel. They were there biddin' on horses as well. Paul Butler's son asked for my permission to come callin' on you."

"Really, Papa?" I responded. See, I was nobody's fool. I knew that it would have been a terrible mistake for me to allow my papa to know just how excited I was. Hell, I was so excited that if anyone had slapped me on my back, I would have peed all over myself.

Papa replied, "Yes, he did ask. Tell me, Margaret, what do you feel about the matter?"

"Well, Papa," I said, "I don't know what to say. It has been a considerable amount of time since we were playin' silly games with each other. As you know, we were mere children. So as I think about it, Papa, I would do best by trustin' your judgment regardin' this matter." Then I almost died from holding my breath as I waited to hear what Papa would say next.

"Margaret, you make your papa so proud because it is wise for a daughter to trust her father to make sound decisions on her behalf. Gabriel does come from a fine family. I have no problems with it, and I believe that I can speak for your mother as well. That is the reason why I told him yes."

It took all I had in me not to jump up and down from excitement, but I managed to remain calm and force out a mere "Thank you, Papa" as I gave him a kiss on the jaw. Later, at the dinner table, Papa did discuss it with Mama, and it gave her as much joy as it did us.

That night, I could not sleep because I was so overwhelmed with excitement, imagining how it would be when Gabriel came to visit—what dress I would be wearing? What colors should I consider, and how would I fix my hair? I could even see him smiling as I dreamed of conversation flowing between us, and at the same time, I was hoping that I would not faint if he kissed my hand. Oh God, how I hoped he would kiss my hand! This was my imagination taking over, but it was all real to me. Why, I was so silly that I even practiced holding out my hand as if he was standing right then and there before me, reaching out in such a gentle way.

I could tell that Mama was happy for me because it made her reminisce about how it was when she and Papa met and the first time he came calling. The look on her face and the joy in her eyes warmed my spirit so, it was as if I could actually see them before me as she talked. She even remembered the dress she wore and shared pieces of the conversation they had. It was so special hearing that my parents had had the same experience. For some reason, we just don't see our parents that way. This was such a sweet time.

Well, Gabriel did come a-calling, and the courtship went well. As expected, on his first visit, I was so nervous, not knowing how things would go, just praying for the best to happen. Life is so funny that way because as a child playing, I'd never given a second thought about what I said or did when it came to Gabriel. But now, even the decision of what I should wear proved to be complicated. I thought that Mama and I had chosen the perfect dress, only to find myself at the last minute changing into something else—all that tension! But the way Gabriel smiled and looked at me when he arrived gave me all the confidence I needed to be myself.

It was good—it was all good. I knew what joy was, but this joy between Gabriel and me brought a spiritual smoothness I had never known. That was the best spring and summer I ever experienced. Our parents were all happy about our courtship. Each Sunday, I looked forward to seeing him in church, but most of all, I looked forward to his visits after church. Those were the times when we would sit on the porch or in the parlor. Many times, he would have dinner with us, and the conversations between him and Papa would always be very interesting. Men did love their talks about politics and business, but these two had a way of keeping Mama and me in the midst of the interaction.

Why, when Gabriel and I were together, we could just simply sit, talk, and laugh for hours on end. I loved the way he would always take time to really listen to me, making me feel most beautiful and secure in our relationship. Gabriel was always a gentleman. Being together, just looking at him and hearing his voice, kept me calm and my spirit at peace. In the past, contentment had always been a stranger, but it was now a familiar friend. Sometimes I felt like stomping my big toe just to see if it was all real and not just a dream.

The holidays were most exciting because we shared them with Gabriel's family. Thanksgiving dinner was at our home, and Christmas dinner was at theirs. After dinner, Gabriel and I ventured into their parlor while our parents continued talking at the dinner table. It was there that we exchanged gifts. For Christmas, I gave Gabriel a very distinguished gold pocket watch that Papa helped me select. I was so excited about my gift for him that I insisted he open it first. I had the words "Special Times" engraved on the back of it.

Looking at the watch, he said, "Margaret, the words are so appropriate because each moment spent with you is special."

Then he gave me my gift, and as I opened it, my breath was taken away because it was the most beautiful and special music box—special because on the day we were reintroduced in the general store, I had seen it and was captivated by it. The store owner wound it up for me, and the sweetest tune, "Breath of Peace" by Joseph Crenshaw, filled the room. Realizing that even back then Gabriel had taken note of me made my heart overflow with such unexpected joy that I screamed, and before I knew it, I hugged and kissed him.

"You remembered, Gabriel! You remembered," I said.

"Yes, that first day in the store, before I recognized who you were, I could not take my eyes off you. I remember the sweetness of your smile as you listened to the music," he said as he held me close to him.

The evening ended with all of us gathered around the piano singing while Mrs. Butler played familiar tunes. Once home and ready for bed, I listened to the sweet sound of the music box, and from then on at bedtime, I would wind it up and listen before going to sleep. I even found it to be calming when I was upset. Then there was the annual Christmas party, where I saved all my dances for Gabriel. That night, it seemed as if Gabriel and

I danced forever. Never before had I experienced such feelings. Gabriel being in my life made everything seem right.

The New Year proved to be unforgettable because Gabriel asked for my hand in marriage. It all took place one Sunday right after the pastor had given the benediction. Then he asked that everyone wait just for one moment before leaving and proceeded to call me up front. The next thing I knew, Gabriel was on one knee before the congregation, asking for my hand in marriage, and of course I said yes.

It turned out that he had already spoken with Papa, and they had agreed to let it be a surprise. The engagement ring was one fit for a queen, and truly it was made known to all at that moment that Margaret was to be Gabriel's queen. Gabriel was really sitting high on the pedestal of my heart.

"It's beginnin' to sprinkle rain," I said to Someday, getting to my feet. "Well, now, Someday, let's go inside because I believe it is goin' to pour down in a minute."

I walked over, opened the screen door, and followed Someday into the house. "Come on, boy, we are goin' to my room. I have somethin' in there I want you to see—somethin' very special."

The two of us entered my bedroom, where I took off my bonnet and laid it on the dresser. I reached for the music box, Someday close up, watching. I wound the music box and opened it, Someday moving backward and barking as the music suddenly started to play.

Softly, I laughed and said, "Now, Someday, there is nothing to be afraid of. It is just sweet music. See, it won't hurt you. Just sweet music." Someday walked a few steps away and lay down, his eyes on me as I sat on the bed and listened to the music box.

4

RUMOR/TRUTH

Finally I found myself being awakened by Someday licking my hand. "Well, boy, I guess between the music and the rain, I went to sleep on you. Please forgive me." I turned on my side to get a good view of Someday.

"Now, what were we talking about? Oh yes, I remember now."

Our special times continued with picnics alone or with our friends, Laura and Edward. We all were children together, but Gabriel went away at a young age to attend school at High Point, and much later, Edward was sent to medical school in England. Unlike Gabriel and me, Laura and Edward stayed in touch by writing. They knew that they loved each other and that someday they were bound to marry— despite the ugly cloud that lingered over Laura's family.

Laura's uncle, her father's brother, had a son name Michael whose mind was not right. They said that he was not born like that. The fact was that Michael was smarter than most of them. He was raised by his grandparents, who, realizing that he was highly intelligent, had given him the best education, ensuring that his future would be very promising. Rumor had it that Michael's father had fallen in love with a woman who was from a lower class of people, and Michael's grandfather would not allow his father to marry her, so they sent their son away, hopin' that he would forget the woman. But instead, Michael's father died of a broken heart, never knowing that the woman was expecting his child.

Even though Michael's mother tried to keep the baby a secret, somehow the grandparents were made aware of his existence. So late one night, they appeared at the woman's door with the authorities, demanding to see the child. Once they saw him, there was no doubt that he was their grandson. It was as if their son had been reborn. Having money and a high status, they used their power to legally take the child and force Michael's mother to leave that town. Michael was raised to believe that his mother had died while birthing him.

What was so shocking about this whole situation was that while touring Europe, some friends had introduced Michael to a brothel that he then began to frequent. It was said that after his third visit, he saw a particular woman who was beautiful to him, even though he could tell that she was older. She had a slim body with long legs and a waist that seemed to invite him to pull her close. Her round face was draped with rich, shiny, black, naturally curly hair that made him want to get lost in it. Enchanting lips were placed perfectly on that face, but something about her eyes made Michael feel as if they did not belong. Those eyes in the middle of all the softness of her face—eyes cold and hardened by a life's mysteries.

He found himself each time asking for only her, and if she was with someone else, he would leave, only to return for her later. For some reason, her eyes haunted him, even at night he could not get her off his mind. They had never really talked before, but one night as he lay with her, he began to ask where she was from—and they learned that they were from the same place. As the conversation continued, the information they shared made the woman realize that Michael was her son—the son taken by force from her arms, the son she continued to dream about, the son she was not allowed to love after losing his father's love. How could life torture her yet again by having her lost son to return in such a manner as this? The shock of it made her rise to her feet, screaming uncontrollably that she was his mother, and then suddenly the horror of the whole situation overtook her, causing her to jump through the glass window and fall to her death.

At first it was thought that he had pushed her. The crazy explanation he gave the authorities of what she had said and done did not make sense and landed him in jail. The news spread fast, and to his amazement, an unknown gentleman came to the jail who was found to be the woman's relative. This was her uncle, her father's brother, whom she had lived with after being forced to leave town. Her uncle informed Michael and the authorities of what Michael's grandfather had done and that unlike his father, who had died from a broken heart, his mother instead had suffered a spiritual death—a death that had driven her into a drunken hell hole of the dark world. She had become a prostitute because life had decided that she wasn't good enough to be part of the world that existed for the only man she loved. Her uncle went on to tell Michael that she had remembered his birthday and hadn't ever stopped loving him and his father, always wishing that she had shared life with them. It was always hard for her to see other women with their babies, especially when the baby was a boy.

Michael was then released from jail to find himself in a state of depression. Still haunted by those cold, hard eyes, he now understood the reason behind the coldness. The impact of what had happened made his friends afraid for him to return home alone, so two of them accompanied him on the journey. Now that the truth had surfaced, he could not stop anticipating returning home to confront his grandfather. Upon his arrival, he confronted the old man, but in the end, he was left with even more animosity because his grandfather still held tight to his self-righteousness.

From then on, Michael slowly sank into a mental darkness. His friends tried to help him overcome the situation by getting him professional help. Michael even tried to move forward by seeking relationships with women, but it was said that everything would be fine until the time of intimacy. In the end, he just could not overcome the ugliness that life had handed him. At times, he would just scream uncontrollably, and he would talk for hours as if having a conversation with his father and mother. Occasionally he would have nightmares of jumping out the window with his mother. His friends realized that his mind would never improve, so they made the decision to commit him to an asylum. After visiting him in the asylum, his grandmother came home and died that night from a heart attack. The doctor said that seeing him locked away was just too much for her to bear.

Some people, being ignorant about the whole situation and sickness of the mind, speculated that it could have been a flaw in the blood line that had caused him to act that way, and if so, other children born in that family could just as well end up crazy. But no matter what people whispered about her family, Edward did not allow that to stop him from loving Laura.

Now that Edward was back, they were engaged, but he needed to complete some things before they set the wedding date. That was another reason it was so much fun spending time with the two of them—we all had similar plans for our lives. Laura and I would sometimes spend hours just chatting about our wedding ideas. But still my heart ached because the freedom and joy I had sharing these things with Miss Sister had been taken away. After a while, I could tell that Miss Sister was trying to force herself to be happy for me. But eventually, a better day came when we both realized how much we missed talking with each other. We could not take it any longer, and so the silence was broken between us.

"Miss Margaret, my heart has been broken because of the death of my hopes of ever jumping the broom with Simon, but I still miss talkin' wit' you bout your weddin'," she said.

I replied, "Oh, Miss Sister, I miss it so much too, but I could not add to your sadness by being so insensitive to your pain. That is why I dared not discuss it anymore."

She told me that she knew I wished the same for her and Simon, but she realized there was nothing I could do. That was just the way things were. The very thought of not being able to marry Gabriel made my sadness for Miss Sister and Simon real. Love was love—it made no difference her being slave or not. Love was just love, and I believe God intended it to be that way.

5

STRAWBERRIES

Well, Someday, after Miss Sister and I were talking to each other again, life went from one exciting moment to the next. The engagement was announced in the paper, which made me the most envied young lady in the town, and everybody who was somebody was at our engagement party. Family members from both our families came from out of town, as well as other friends and associates, to be part of the gala affair. This was when I had the pleasure of meeting Bunny—Miss Bunny Boaderwright, cousin to Gabriel, the daughter of Judge Butler's sister. I could tell right off that she admired Gabriel and desired deep down to be more than just a cousin, but since that could not be, she had decided to be my terror for that night. She would soon learn that she was no match for me.

I could never forget how she looked that evening when the Boaderwrights arrived—tall and slender with dark brown hair, wearing a beautiful lavender gown accented with breathtaking jewelry, holding tightly on to Gabriel's arm as if she was Miss Somebody. It was a pleasure meeting her parents; but when Gabriel introduced us, Bunny looked me straight in my eyes as if to challenge me. Early on, I noticed how she was watching us, and she would seize every opportunity to find a way to get close to Gabriel when I was not around, whispering in his ears and making him laugh at God knows what. My friends Calvin and Josh were there, and when I confided in them, they assured me that the situation would be taken care of. Calvin danced with her, and afterward, when he led her to her seat, Josh made sure that she sat on some strawberries. Later, when someone else took her hand and escorted her to the dance floor, her mother rushed up beside her to make it known that her dress was stained. It was so embarrassing—so much so that she refused Mama's offer to fit her in one of my dresses. She left, and not a minute too soon. Thanks to God for Calvin and Josh, Gabriel and I had a wonderful evening. After that I always smiled whenever I saw strawberries.

Mama and I had so much fun planning everything, but when it came time to choose my wedding gown, she and I had the worst fight ever. I began to wonder if it was my wedding or Mama's. You see, I had always dreamed of my dress being my favorite color buttercup yellow. Mama would not hear of it.

She said, "White is the traditional wedding gown color for a virgin. My grandmama wore white, your grandmama wore white, and I, your Mama, wore white—and that, my dear, is what you are goin' to wear. Margaret, you will not disgrace your father and me. Think, girl. Do you ever think about how people would gossip? Especially our own family members! They would be whisperin' behind our backs while smilin' in our faces. And all sorts of questions would be dancin' in the minds of the church folks!"

"I don't give a hoot about what people think," I replied. "This will be my affair. Those who don't like it can stay at home for all I care."

But she would not let it go. "Do you want Gabriel to be embarrassed by thoughts of him marryin' a whore?" She didn't really win that fight; I just surrendered because of Gabriel. So instead we had a special dress made for the wedding rehearsal that was buttercup yellow.

I never imagined that being in the center of attention could be so exhausting for the bride. There were the bridal showers given by the church, another by my friends, and of course one by all the women in Gabriel's and my families. It was one big gathering after another, and considering all the planning for everything, at times it was overwhelming, causing me to be very fussy at times.

But Gabriel and I did survive it all. The wedding was like something written in a fairy tale. Laura was my bridesmaid, and Edward was Gabriel's best man. Papa looked most handsome when he escorted me down the aisle. During the ceremony, it was as if I was in a daze, and the only thing that brought me back to reality was saying our *I do*s.

On my wedding night, having intercourse for the first time was a horrible ordeal and not what I had envisioned it to be—not only the pain of him bursting into me down there, which left me feeling all awkward and such, but also the soreness that remained several days thereafter. I told Gabriel that I felt as if someone had driven a team of horses up my behind, and that now I understood the term intercourse—because he surely had entered my ass. Now I was wondering why it was so important for the bed sheets to be white.

"Gabriel, this was not what I bargained for," I said, looking at him in a confused state. "Are you sure you know what you are doin'?" But he explained that it was only because it was the first time for me. He promised that each time thereafter it would be much better. He was right because after that, things seemed to flow well between Gabriel and me. I guess you could call it a match made in heaven. I was glad that I had remained a virgin until marriage—that I had waited for Gabriel. Now my body was vowed to him and him only until death departed us.

Now sitting up on the side of the bed, I said to Someday, "Let's go outside. There is nothin' better than a walk after rain. Don't you agree, boy?"

6

WANTING TO HATE MISS SISTER

Once Someday and I were back outside, we began to walk the property.

Gabriel and his family did well in preparing our new home for us. The transition was a smooth one, even though I have to admit that it was hard leaving my parents and the only home I had ever known. But Miss Sister's coming with us helped to ease my pain. Now, her pain was a different matter. She'd walk around looking like the living dead, and other times, for no reason, she'd burst into tears, and I would find myself tryin' to console her.

"Now, now Miss Sister, I keep remindin' you to look at it this way—things could be worse. Papa could have sold you off to some mean family to die from workin' hard in the field. I know you don't have Simon, but you do have me, Miss Sister, and God knows that I do love you," I would say to her.

In the beginning we were quite busy, going to dinner at different family members' homes, being entertained by town officials, and fellowshipping with the church members. Our first dinner party included the pastor, the bank manager, the mayor, and their wives. I made sure that everything was perfectly done. The menu was carefully selected and the food prepared well. The table setting was immaculately done—fit for a king and queen. I even hired a pianist to play while we dined. Gabriel was so proud of me. Mama always said that the wife's greatest responsibility was to assist her husband in standing proudly before the people—never tearing him down, but always building him up.

The elite community really embraced us. I became a part of the quilting group, and the wives of the town's top businessmen invited me to be a part of their fund-raising committee. Throughout the year they would plan functions, such as art exhibits, classical music concerts, ballroom dancing, and other gatherings. The money would be used for the betterment of the town, including paying for teachers' salaries and school supplies and funding the hospital. It was so exciting to be recognized in the social arena. It kept me busy, making sure that I stayed informed about the latest in women garments. Looking my very best was the order of each day.

Tradition would've had me just wait until my husband wanted to be intimate because it was deemed sinful for a lady to request it. Gabriel and I would always fight about my requesting it, even though when we got to it, he was just as passionate as I was. I made my request known to him any time of day or night. He said that he never knew a white woman like me, wanting to have intercourse during the day instead of waiting for the proper time at night. He went on to say that he knew Mama was such a proper lady and that she had taught me the right way regarding such matters. He concluded that I was just plain stubborn. But hell, I did not care—all I knew was that I enjoyed kissing him until he reached that point of no return, and with a loss of control, he would mount me from the front. I'd watch the expression of wildness on his face as he continuously thrust inward, and then, with no warning, he would quickly turn me over and enter me from behind, giving me a ride of passion. I always had to have it. I found it to be the best thing God created for man and woman—truly heaven on earth.

Suddenly our intimacy was not important to Gabriel any more. I began to notice how he would stay up and send me to bed all alone. At first I would go on to sleep so that when he came to bed I would be rested and ready to make passionate love. Instead, I would be awakened by him trying to ease into bed. I would try to draw close to him, kissing and caressing him, just to be pushed away with some excuse as to why it was not a good time. And the times that he would accept my affection, it felt as if it was only because of his marital obligation. This rejection continued, and night after night, I would cry myself to sleep as my body burned for him. I craved to feel his hands wildly exploring me until he would finally enter me with an erection that awakened my soul, his deep, passionate kisses almost taking my breath away, taking me higher and higher until we reached that heavenly place of ecstasy as he explored inside me. Then we would collapse, drained in peace—knowing that nothing was held back, that all was given and all was released.

Finally I needed to know what he was doing. Was he leaving the house after I went to sleep, and if so, where was he going? So one night I decided to stay awake. I even went so far as to make him think that I was not feeling well and warmed some milk to help me sleep. I waited, and sure enough, after an hour or so, he came up stairs and softly called my name. When I did not answer, he closed the door and went back down the steps. I heard him leave out the back door, ran to the other side of the house, and looked out the window. My eyes followed him.

I knew that something was not right. What was it, and why was it so? When I saw where he was going, I could not believe it. It was as if my heart had burst out of my chest and the final breath of life was trying to leave. He crossed the backyard, past the clotheslines and straight into Miss Sister's room. It was unbelievable, but I knew that, yes, I had to believe it. Breathing hard and gasping for control, I finally made it down the stairs, and the next thing I knew, I was at the foot of Miss Sister's bed, watching Gabriel riding her, giving her everything I wanted from him. At that moment, I did not care about being a gentle southern lady. I had to fight and maybe kill for what was mine.

I became as a wildcat, jumping on Gabriel's back, hitting, scratching, and biting. Eventually I found myself getting off the floor. I guess Gabriel had thrown me off. Now, as he stood naked over me, I jumped back, with all my focus on getting to Miss Sister. I needed to kill her—I had too. But then I saw her tear-stained face and heard her pain-filled voice as she cried out, "Miss Margaret, please make him leave me alone. Can't you make Master stop?" At that time, Gabriel slapped her to the floor with his right hand and pushed me back with his left.

"You're nothin' but what I say you are, gal," he said to Miss Sister. Then looked at me, his eyes filled with disgust, and said, "And you, Margaret, you disgrace yourself as a white woman. No lady wants done to her what I do to this gal." And as he gathered his pants, he shouted, "Hear me! I am the master, and like it or not, both of y'all will do just as I say, you, Margaret, as my wife, and you as my slave. I own the both of you."

Then he pulled on his trousers, gathered his clothes, and slammed the door behind him before rushing out into the darkness, leaving us in disbelief. For the first time in my life, I wanted to hate Miss Sister, but I was still trying to comprehend all that my husband had just done and said.

It was an ugly silence that lasted too long, but Miss Sister finally broke it. "Can't you make him stop, Miss Margaret? I don't like him touchin' me down there. Please make Master stop. I have begged him and begged him. But Master keeps right on comin'."

And then all I could do was grab her and hug her as the pain connected our spirits—a pain that became larger than the two of us, consuming the whole room, a pain that left no hope for peace. *Oh pain, pain, go away, and don't come back another day …*

7

LOST IDENTITY

I stopped for a moment and looked down at my dog. "Someday, I know you don't understand any of this, but it gives me great relief to talk it out."

Regarding this matter, nothing changed, and so sadness filled my life, swelled up in my throat. I could not sleep, let alone eat. I had become so thin when Gabriel suggested that maybe a visit back home would be like a dose of much-needed medicine. Ah, to see Mama and Papa. I wondered if they could bring some order, maybe even recapture the escaped peace. Peace. Peace, did I know you? Did I ever have you? Or were you always an illusion?

Maybe I could have understood the situation if I had been that timid little wife, cold and withdrawn in spirit, always refusing him. Instead, I was not fearful, but rather eager to explore all the possibilities of satisfying him and myself as well. This was the one thing that had given me complete joy, as well as the satisfaction in knowing that Gabriel's body was mine to have.

Now realty had come, so cruelly, leaving me frozen and not knowing who I was. My identity was gone, stolen by his desire for another. Never again was I to be that woman who had power over her man in bed; never again would I take him up to the third heavens. Ours was a passion so sweet, but so explosive—passion leading, and yet being led, reaching calmness while creating a rhythm of wildness. This was such torture!

Gone, all gone, so suddenly, and in its place I found compassion. Compassion was born because now I understood Miss Sister's pain. Now I understood the pain of being locked away from love, the pain of having to satisfy the desires of the unwanted. I decided that there had to be a way to fight Gabriel. So I made the decision that when Miss Sister and I visited Mama and Papa, I would make sure that she got to spend one night with her lost love.

On the morning we left, Miss Sister was so excited that a glimmer of life sparkled in her eyes—those beautiful black eyes that had gone from demanding to just accepting. I realized just how much she missed her mama and Simon. Of course, my leaving home was different because I had married the man I loved. Our lives had just begun as husband and wife, so the anticipation of all that satisfied my want for Mama and Papa.

I see now just how selfish I was, for I only briefly considered Miss Sister's feelings. At first I had tried to get Papa to change his mind and allow Miss Sister to stay and jump the broom with Simon. But Papa had decided that Miss Sister would be a wedding gift to Gabriel. Only men could own property. Looking back, I wondered—was his giving Miss Sister to Gabriel a secret between men for bed privileges?

But at that moment, I just saw it as being what was normal for a slave. No matter what, it was their duty to serve the master, and besides, she was going to be with me, which was always a good thing for me—or so I thought. Had I really thought that, or was it just my way of conveniently moving on? It did not matter that as I was planning my wedding she was looking forward to jumping the broom with Simon. It did not matter that my getting married would force her to be separated from everything and everybody that brought her joy. And it did not matter that I was becoming a wife and Miss Sister was becoming a house nigger. Compassion—things always look different when the cost is not yours to pay.

8

SHAMEFUL FOR A WOMAN TO DISCUSS

As Someday and I walked, I stopped to pick a couple of blackberries to eat.

Our trip home was much needed. Miss Sister and I started out crying, but later, for some reason, we stopped and stared at each other, and from then on, we found ourselves laughing and talking so much that the long hours passed by.

After that nine-hour ride, we finally reached home feeling dirty from the long, dusty trail. A nice, long, hot bath was the immediate goal on my mind. Mama was there waiting with relief and joy when her eyes found me. Gabriel had sent word letting them know that I was coming. To my disappointment, Papa had gone off to take care of some important business, but he was expected to return in about two weeks. After all that had taken place, I knew that I could survive waiting for his return.

Aging had made Mama seem so frail. She was always a woman strong with sunshine energy. I noticed that when she looked at Miss Sister, an unexpected sadness was there. Immediately she called for Ruth and Lessie to come help Miss Sister carry her things to the backhouse where her mama lived.

"What is wrong, Mama?" I asked.

Mama, feelin' faint, braced herself against one of the columns on the porch. Mama began to explain that Cora, Miss Sister's mama, had been sick and died a few days ago. Moments later, I heard a deafening scream. Quickly, I ran to the backhouse, where Ruth and Lessie were trying to calm Miss Sister. I pushed through to reach for her, but Miss Sister refused to be comforted, fighting our outstretched hands that wanted to hold her. Finally, her back pressed against the wall, she slid to the floor, hugging herself, and began patting her ears to shut out our words. There was no comforting her. The only decent thing we could do now was to allow her the respect of being alone to digest this new pain.

Miss Sister's mama was gone now, and once again, this life she was destined to live had made its decision—just as it had decided to deny her the experience of Simon's love. Simon was the one person she had given her heart to, but never gave her body; Simon was the one whose wife she always dreamed of being and whose babies she longed to have; Simon was the ultimate desire of her spirit. Now she was left asking why she had not been allowed the chance to be there when her mama passed. She was left to wonder what her mama's last thoughts were, what her last words were, if she asked for her child—her only child. How cruel, when the essence of living was to love and be loved. To live without love was to exist in a never-ending hell—a hell that seemed to grow continuously for Miss Sister. There were no more tears to shed, and that was all right because life did not respect her tears.

Hours had passed, and Miss Sister lay there with tear-stained face, hair, and bed. Her eyes were swollen in disbelief, her hands clenched in fear of what was to come; her body was limp from despair. Strength was now a stranger.

I knew that now more than ever that she needed Simon. I sent for him, and at sunset, Miss Sister was awaken by a gentle tap at the door, followed by a voice she had longed to hear—a voice that could soothe the deepness of her pains. It was Simon.

"Violet, Violet." The voice was whispering her name so sweetly. At the same time, the door was opening and the flickering of the candlelight exposed her eyes to a silhouette of love. In a matter of seconds, love stood before her, encased in the smoothness of rich black skin.

"Simon, my mama! My mama, Simon!" she said with outstretched arms.

"I know, Violet," said Simon. Then he picked her up in his arms and held her in his lap like a baby.

"I know," he whispered again, softly. As she was pressed against his chest, her head locked under his chin, she began to feel the moisture of his tears. It was as if he knew her pain had emptied her of tears, and so he wept for her.

After a while of sitting there in silence, Simon gathered water in the washbowl and began washing her face, kissing her tenderly as he did. Finally, with both hands, she grabbed his shirt and pulled him close and kissed him as if her life depended on it. Their bodies pressed together, they fell back onto the bed. Their kisses called for more as her hands wildly explored his body, undressing him while his hands did the same to her. But just at that passionate moment, reality crept in and reminded her that life had even stolen the promise of her body.

"No, no, no, Simon," she said. "Won't allow nobody to make you second. Master Gabe already been here. He took my body. They wouldn't let us marry—they took that from us too. I love you so much, Simon. Won't have you be second to no white man."

Simon was quiet because reality set in, and he knew that it was for the best. Violet would be gone soon. He did not want to take the chance of her gettin' pregnant by him. Life for them was already a burning and smothering hell, and that would add more fuel to the fire. So now silence was their portion for the rest of the night.

* * *

After leaving Miss Sister, I went in the house to be refreshed with a long, hot bath, and just like old times, Mama brushed my hair afterward. She even kissed me on my forehead. It was so soothing having the love and attention of my mama—which was what brought my heart and thoughts back to Cora and Miss Sister.

"Mama, do you know what was wrong with Cora? Did she suffer long?" I asked.

She replied, "Some kind of poisonin' in her body, the doctor said—but you know, Margaret, that I am not good with rememberin' medical words. All I know is it started with coughin', and then a fever set in for about three days, and then she died. It made her foolish in the head; she did not know anyone. As a matter of fact, she stopped talkin' altogether."

After all was silent between us, I asked, "Has it been hard for you, now that she is gone? I mean, I cannot bear the thought of losin' Miss Sister."

"Yes, I do miss her," Mama replied. "Only God knows just how much. Why, just the other mornin' as I was wakin' up, I found myself callin' for her, but quickly I gathered my senses when there was no response. All those years of callin' her name, and before I could finish callin', she would come in a hurry to see what was wanted. Margaret, I really depended on Cora. I even tried to think back and could not remember a day of her not bein' with us. I still cannot believe she is no more. All those years of service—guess it is sort of like losin' a family member. Why, come to think of it, she helped me set up house when your papa and I first married, and she was right here helpin' the doctor when you were born. She even took care of your great-grandma Lizzie before she died. I never had to worry about things bein' done right because Cora had a way with the other servants—such a way that all she had to do was look at them and tell them once what was needed, and all was taken care of. Why, I think they respected her maybe more than me or your papa."

I interrupted, "Mama, just now I was rememberin' Cora's laugh. When she laughed, it was so hearty that it made you stop and watch to see if she would survive it."

"That's right, Margaret. No one could laugh like Cora. Why, I remember when you were about five years old, and Ruddy was ..." Her voice trailed off, and with a sudden sadness, she said, "Now Ruth has taken over those matters, and even though she is doing a fine job and she has been with us for a long while, it is just strange, just simply strange. She is no Cora."

Later, Mama tucked me in and had food brought up to the room. It was just like Mama to make sure I had all my favorite foods. I was so overjoyed with this surprise that I did not know where to begin. After all I had gone through, it was surprising to see that I had an appetite. While I ate, Mama tried to bring me up to date with the town gossip. She told me of how Deacon Martin had died while in bed with one of the town whores and that Jeff Adams had several of his slaves run off one night while they were having a big Christmas celebration. They never captured them. Not a one.

"Mama, why do there have to be slaves?" I asked.

"Margaret, what has gotten into you, child? That's a man's business, no concern for us ladies," she said.

"Why, Mama?" I asked.

But I reckon I was speaking to the wind because Mama continued on to tell me that Mr. and Mrs. Jim Murray had finally had a little boy after having seven girls and that there was a big celebration on his first birthday. Mr. Murray owned the largest plantation and worried that he would have no son to leave it to. But now God had been generous and granted him his desire. Mama said she had never seen a happier man.

"Mama, does Papa regret that I was not born a boy?" I asked.

"Hush, Margaret. How could you think such a thing? You are your Papa's pride and joy. You know he would do anything for you, child, or die tryin'," she said. "And besides, we could have no finer son than Gabriel. You married well, Margaret. I am so proud of you."

We continued talking, and after much laughter and many questions asked and answered, Mama suddenly stopped and looked deep into my eyes.

"What is wrong, Margaret?" she asked, gently rubbing my left arm. "Don't try to pretend that it's nothin'. At first I thought it was just the tiredness from that long, dusty travel. I am your Mama and I know my child."

At that moment, it was if a beaver's dam had broken, and I found myself cryin' with no end in sight. "Mama, Gabriel has been sleepin' with Miss Sister. I saw him with my own eyes. I don't understand how he could do this to me."

"Why, Margaret," she interrupted in shock, "I taught you to be a lady."

"Mama, you told me that I would not like havin' intercourse with my husband, but Mama, it is the most wonderful feelin'."

Eyes wide with disbelief, she said, "Hush, Margaret. Some things are not to be discussed. I never raised you to act like no beast."

"But Mama—" I said.

"Hush, Margaret," she said.

But I continued, "That's the most wonderful feelin' I have ever experienced."

"Hush! You hush right now!" Mama yelled.

"How could you not love Papa in that way?"

Next I thought I had been struck by lightning, realizing later it was Mama slapping me.

Then, while shaking me, she ended the conversation with "Hush, Margaret. I don't know what has gotten into you. Some things are a sin before God and shameful for a lady to discuss." And that was that.

9

MY PARENTS' HEARTS REVEALED

Now Someday and I found ourselves at the lake, where, after throwing a couple of rocks in the water, I sat on a bench. Someday looked at me as if to tell me to continue talking. I held him under his chin and smiled, looking him in the eyes to acknowledge him as I started to reflect again.

After two days of visiting with other family members, shopping, and having friends over for tea and tea cakes, I decided to visit my in-laws, the Butlers. I felt that the trip would be refreshing for Mama as well, so I invited her to accompany me. She accepted my invitation only if I promised not to bring up the matter regarding Gabriel. Wanting so much for this to be a pleasant time for us, I promised. Besides, I had not given up hope that Papa would set things straight when he returned.

The Butlers were so happy to have us as their guests, but they noticed right off that sadness filled my eyes. I told them it was just that I missed Gabriel so much, and they settled for that explanation. Then they went on to say how much they were hoping that soon we would make them proud grandparents. They even made it known that this was one of their daily prayers. Of course, my Mama agreed wholeheartedly.

They really went all out to show us the fineness of their hospitality, making sure that Mama and I had our favorite foods to eat. Even Miss Sister seemed to enjoy the change. She and Flora, Mrs. Butler's personal maid, appeared to get along well. Mrs. Butler took us to the best shops in town, and Mama and I bought gifts for Papa and Gabriel. We attended a couple of social events that brought out many of the town's high-standing citizens, and each night at dinner, there were other guests. We did so much while visiting the Butlers that the time to return home found Mama and me looking forward to getting back so we could just do nothing for a change—and that was what we did.

My papa finally returned from his business trip. I looked out the window of the sittin' room and saw Papa's carriage coming. I jumped to my feet because at that moment, the only thing that mattered was for me to spend all my energy trying to get outside so I could have my papa's eyes set upon me—those eyes that made me feel safe from all of the world's harm. I needed so much to feel safe again.

Before Papa's feet could touch the ground, I was in his arms, and as we hugged, I felt like a little girl. Now I was safe and I knew it. Life had taught me that this was the only man who would always love me; nothing could tarnish a daddy's love for his little girl. I would always be Papa's little girl—how sweet, how safe, how secure with my Papa.

As we stood looking at each other, Papa gave me a big kiss on my forehead and said, "Margaret, what's wrong with you? Why, child, there is such sadness in your eyes. I expected to see these eyes filled with the joy of a newlywed. Now, Gabriel will have to take better care of you, darling." By this time Mama had walked out to join us.

I explained, "Papa, I love Gabriel, but he is sleepin' with Miss Sister, and I don't know what to do. Tell me what I should do, Papa."

This was the first time I ever saw my papa at a loss for words.

Then, suddenly, his face turned red from embarrassment, and he said in disbelief, "Elizabeth, it appears that you have not done such a good job teaching our daughter her place as a lady—hell, as a wife! These are issues discussed amongst women behind closed doors."

"Andrew, I have had this conversation with Margaret—as a matter of fact, the first night she got here," Mama explained. "But she is just too stubborn to listen."

I began to raise my voice. "So, Papa, you are in agreement with this. I just knew that you would make things right. You always made me feel secure. So I am not supposed to enjoy being intimate with my husband? I am supposed to accept that he is an adulterer?"

"God damn it, Margaret, he's no adulterer!" Papa yelled. "That's a mere slave! She is that man's property, and he can do whatever he wants because he owns her."

I continued raising my voice, trying so hard to get them to hear me. I just needed to get somebody to hear me—and then I was sure that things would be put right. "I enjoy making love with my husband. I enjoy it so much that I crave having him between my legs."

"Shut up, Margaret! Please say no more," Mama cried, gasping for breath.

"So this is what the men do? This is what you do, Papa? I will not continue to share my husband. I just will not. There has to be a way to put a stop to this!" I ran into the house, leaving them in total confusion.

That night, we had guests for dinner: my uncle John, Papa's brother, and his wife, Aunt Hilda. They would stay for a couple of days. I had not seen them since my wedding, and I was really looking forward to their visit. Mama, Aunt Hilda, and I always had wonderful times together. Aunt Hilda really knew how to make me feel special. I think she loved being with me because they only had three sons. With me, she got to experience having a girl around to do some of the things that mothers and daughters did. I could get away with a lot when she was around.

I could recall one instance in particular when I was a young girl. I was visiting them when, late one night, I could not sleep and decided that I would slip out of the house to sit on the porch and watch the moon. I always enjoyed moon watching. Many times back home Papa and I would sit and watch the moon while he chewed on leftover meat from dinner, and to make it special for me, he would give me candy.

Well, that night, I got out the bed and eased out the room carefully, not wanting to wake anybody. The house was so quiet, but as I closed the door and turned around, I found my little cousin Frank coming down the hall with cake in his hand. Quickly, I put my hand over his mouth and then led him down the stairs, out of the house, and onto the porch.

"Why did you bring me out here, Margaret?" he whispered.

"To look at the moon, boy. Why, there ain't nothin' prettier than that," I said as I pointed to it. "So full, sittin' up there in the wide-open sky."

Well, while sitting on the steps eating the stolen cake in the quiet of the night, we began hearing noises coming from Uncle John and Aunt Hilda's room.

"Frank, I guess we better go back to bed before we get in trouble," I whispered. As we were tiptoeing up the steps and past their room, we heard them again—and, knowing better but just being foolish, I quickly opened their bedroom door and pushed Frank in. I slammed the door behind him and ran to my room.

Boy, I could hear Frank being yelled at as he fearfully tried to explain and Uncle John was jumping out the bed onto the floor. After all the yelling and screaming settled down, Aunt Hilda came to my room. Soon as she opened the door, I ran over and threw my arms around her waist and buried my face in her gown.

"Well, now, young lady, tell me—why did you do that? For what reason did you push Frank into our room?" she asked as she pulled away so she could look me straight in my face.

"Aunt Hilda, I thought Uncle John was fightin' you, so bein' scared and all, I pushed Frank into your room so him bein' a boy could make him stop hurtin' you," I said, knowing it was all just a lie.

She began to laugh, and, after hugging me, she said, "Why, Margaret, child, your uncle John loves your aunt Hilda and will never do anythin' to hurt me. We were just playin' a game for grownups. Now you stop fretting and go to bed." Then she helped me into bed and gave me a kiss on my head while covering me up.

She saved my behind from a well-deserved whipping, and I, being so relieved at the outcome, was ready to go to sleep. I fell asleep with a smile on my face because I knew that Aunt Hilda knew that I was lying.

That night, when Uncle John and Aunt Hilda came to visit, Miss Sister was helping serve the food. As she served Uncle John, he placed his hand on her arm and looked up at her with misbehaving eyes. "Well, now, is this Cora's child?" he asked, a sneaky smile on his face.

"Yes, sir," she answered.

"My, my, my, Miss Sister, the last time I saw you, gal, was when Margaret got married. Yes, that's right—you reside with Gabriel and Margaret now."

I could see the lust gleaming in his eyes as he looked her up and down. Before I could think this matter through, words were rushing out my mouth like soldiers rushing to battle.

"I guess now, Uncle John, *you* want to take her to bed?"

"Why, Margaret!" he exclaimed.

Papa hit the table with his hand, Mama almost choked on her water, and Aunt Hilda began to fan her face with the dinner napkin as if the room had suddenly become hot. Miss Sister ran out into the kitchen.

"Why not? That is what Gabriel does. Is that what you do? Tell us—do you do the same as our other white men? Take the slaves to bed because we white ladies are too fragile for intercourse with our own husbands, too clean for perspiring and such?" I cried. Mama began to cry.

"Why, I never …" said Aunt Hilda, disgusted.

"You never what, Aunt Hilda?" I asked.

"In all my life, I have never heard a lady say such things," she said, looking at my Mama.

At the same time, my papa was shoutin' to the top of his voice, "Margaret, I demand that you excuse yourself from this table right now!" Uncle John was so shocked that he turned fire red and could not say another word.

"Aunt Hilda, do you agree that we are not to enjoy it?" I asked as I got up to leave the room. As I left, I wondered whether she would have felt compelled to give me an answer if I had stayed a little longer.

Peace had abandoned us, and we were left to contend with a restless night. It was not my intention to upset everyone, but this silent monster had to be confronted and dealt with, even if nothing changed. It had been exposed, and my only hope was that they would eventually realize that it existed and that this wrong needed to be made right. Maybe it was too late for Mama and Aunt Hilda, but not for my generation.

Back with Someday, I turned to the dog and said, "Miss Sister did get to have that last night with Simon."

* * *

Overwhelmed with all that happened at dinner and the fleetingness of time, Miss Sister lay still, her head on Simon's chest. These were her thoughts: *No time to allow regrets to fill these precious moments—these precious, last moments. Just lie right here and think on Simon's presence, a presence of calmness, a presence of thankfulness, and a presence of real love. We only shared this love for a short time, but it had the power to heal beyond eternity. This man is so gentle, so caring, and so consumed by peace.*

In those precious moments, they shared looks, her big, beautiful eyes taking him into her heart and spirit. He kissed her hands with lips of warmness—hands that had worked hard for her master, cooking, cleaning, and digging. But his kisses made those hands contemplate beauty in spite of the hardness of life. Their embrace defied separation. Now his head lay in her bosom as if it was a familiar place, and in this place was a softness that soothed the pain of what was to come. In this visit she had experienced the loss of her mother, her only known relative. But in those moments with Simon, she experienced life as ignited by Simon's love. Love was a stranger that she had longed to meet, but she hadn't dared to hope for such a time as this.

"Right now is all we have, Violet, but I thank God for right now," Simon whispered in the darkness of the night. "This, right now, will take me through 'til death comes callin'."

* * *

Early that mornin', I heard Uncle John and Aunt Hilda leavin'—I guess they were too embarrassed to stay any longer. Not knowin' if that was the end of that conversation, it was best to leave before breakfast and avoid a repeat of what had taken place at dinner. I too, decided it was best not to stay for the length of time I'd planned. There was too much tension between Papa, Mama, and me. They would not change their minds, and I would not allow them to change mine. Nothing was settled; all I had now was the hope that God would have Gabriel see my pain and love me enough that he would no longer follow in the footsteps of our fathers.

Papa had gotten up early that morning and left. I am sure it was to keep from seeing me after the embarrassment I had caused last night. But Mama was there, and as we walked out to the carriage, she began to explain. "Margaret, dear, right now you refuse to understand how things go. But I am hopin' that one day you will come to understand that we always do what is best for you."

"How was Papa giving Miss Sister as a gift to Gabriel for bed privileges best for me, Mama?" I asked.

"It was best that Miss Sister not be allowed to marry because then it would have been more important for her to look after her husband than for her to take care of you," Mama replied.

"Takin' care of me, or takin' care of my husband?" I said.

"One thing for sure is that Miss Sister has always loved and took care of you, even when you were children, and what was done was and still is what is best for you, Margaret," she explained.

"Best for me," I said. "Mama, you say I will come to understand that." Suddenly the tone of my voice changed to reflect the anger in my heart. "Never as long as I live will I understand this, and all I can wish for is that the day will come when I can forgive Papa for what he has done."

Mama gave me a look of disbelief. "No, Margaret, your papa only decided to give Gabriel a slave. Blame me for suggestin' that it be Miss Sister."

I was so devastated by that revelation that before I knew it, I had slapped my dear mama.

When I came to myself, Miss Sister and I were in the carriage and had been riding for a while. I began to cry out, "I just can't believe that Mama did this to me!" Suddenly, as I looked up at Miss Sister, I screamed so loud, "She did this to us! Mama did this to both of us, Miss Sister."

But Miss Sister never said a word. She didn't have to—I could see the anguish on her face and the pain and despair in her eyes. I realized that she was numb from all that had happened during our visit home—the passing of her mother, seeing Simon just to leave him again, and now this. At that moment I reached out to comfort her.

It was a long journey home, and the thickness of the silence in the carriage weighed heavily upon us. We knew that no matter how much this hurt, the reality was there was nothing we could do about the matter. I had mixed emotions about seeing Gabriel—love and hate. I never would have imagined our lives being tortured by such darkness. I had hoped that my visit home would make things better for us, but now I was returning and all was worse. Finding out the truth of the matter and leaving Mama in such a state of shock.

I was so glad that it was dark when we arrived home so I could blame my rushing to bed on my tiredness from the trip. Surprisingly, later that night, Gabriel came to bed and reached out to me for intimacy. Even though I was still angry and mentally drained from all that had happened, I did not refuse him for fear he would leave my bed and go to Miss Sister's. What had once been my joy was now my wifely duty. My hope was that the good Lord would allow the morning to bring me the strength I needed to handle my life.

10

HORRORS OF LIFE SPILL OUT

After crying over my story with Someday, I realized I needed to go on and get it all out.

Days passed, and still there was a burning in my heart for things to be resolved. Gabriel wanted to know all about my visit home, how our families were, and what news I had of Edward and Laura. Of course, I had to avoid the unpleasant moments I had caused. I knew that it would only make matters worse, and besides, there was no end to it in sight. So I began to look forward to Sunday. We always went to church on Sunday—me in my fashionable hats and my Sunday best, with colors that made you think of picking flowers on a summer day. Gabriel, being the handsome man he was, always made me so proud being escorted by him. Every Sunday was like an Easter parade with the women watching to see who was wearing what, fueling conversations for that whole week. We would arrive early to gather outside and talk with other church members before the service began.

Just before going into the church Luke and Bessie, along with their daughter, Mae Ella, shared their joy regarding Mae Ella being asked for her hand in marriage. She was their oldest of five children: three girls and two boys. They had been preparing her for this time in her life, and they had done well—her fiancé was the son of Judge Clifford Palmer, patriarch of one of the most prominent families. You knew that everybody who was somebody would be invited to the engagement celebration. This would give the women somethin' else to look forward to. It would truly be a time of high fashion, especially for the other young women who hoped to soon be engaged. But on this particular Sunday, Reverend Parkinson was teaching from the eighth chapter of John. Years later, I could still see him, standing in the pulpit in that gray suit, the size of one and a half men. His vest was buttoned all the way up while his stomach looked as if it was crying to be set free. He was preaching, and as you heard his voice shouting, you felt as if Jesus was soon to be a-coming back.

[John 8:1-5] "Jesus went unto the Mount of Olives. And early in the morning he came again into the temple, and all the people came unto him; and he sat down, and taught them. And the scribes and Pharisees brought unto him a woman taken in adultery; and when they had set her in the midst, They say unto him, Master, this woman was taken in adultery, in the very act. Now Moses in the law commanded us, that such should be stoned: but what sayest thou?"

Before I knew it, I had jumped to my feet, shouting, "But what says God, Reverend Parkinson, about a married man sleepin' with his slave woman?"

Reverend Parkinson, not believing what was taking place, continued on:

[John 8:6] "This they said, tempting him that they might have to accuse him."

"But what says God, Reverend Parkinson, about a married man sleepin' with his slave woman?" I yelled out again. "Tell me, Reverend Parkinson, and all y'all married men in here, what y'all think about a married man sleepin' with his slave woman and denyin' his wife of such humanly pleasures."

Gabriel began to pull me out into the aisle as I fought back. Still I was determined to have my say, crying, "I tell you, it is adultery. Adultery, I say, and a shame before God."

The only thing you could hear now was Mother Jenkins as she fainted and fell to the floor and the hurried steps of those running to help her. Reverend Parkinson asked, "Brother Gabriel, can't you handle your wife?"

The next thing I knew, Gabriel had thrown me across his back and was carrying me from the church. All the while, I was kicking and yelling, "I demand an answer! Somebody answer me!"

The choir began to sing loud enough for heaven to hear them. I could see others' eyes as they watched—eyes whispering their disbelief that I had released the unmentionable, something so powerful that it had to stay imprisoned in their minds for fear that if it reached the lips, it would become ugliness settled in the heart. But I released it to the wind. Who had created it, and why was it not aborted, but allowed to live?

Once outside the church, I cried so hard that Gabriel pulled me close to him. I believed that in that moment he really felt my pain as he rubbed my hair softly while my head lay on his chest. His gentleness recalled to my memory the Gabriel I had first married.

"Hush, Margaret. Hush, sweetheart," he said, trying to ease this pain that he had not protected me from. Gabriel tried to get me to understand that it was just the way of being a man. But while he talked, my mind confronted God with the issue.

God, you created them. Men—are they not supposed to protect us women? Men are so different in their thinkin' and their ways of doin' things. God, what is it that I am supposed to understand about Gabriel? What am I to accept? To love is to trust, but how can I trust this? Love is supposed to be patient, love is kind, but how am I to be patient with Gabriel's unkindness? Love does not envy, it does not boast, it is not proud; but Lord, I do envy the thought of him touchin'

SANDRA COOPER

another woman. Yes, I did say woman—even though my world would have me see Miss Sister as a nigger, less than human.

Lord, what sin did I commit that brought this pain to me? Did I overly enjoy our intimacy and so was deemed boastful and full of pride? I think not. I am the one who has been dishonored. My God, don't you see that the men are at fault here and are guilty of self-seekin' pleasures at the cost of our pain? I cannot believe that I am the only white woman who has been angered, her spirit left in bitterness by the wrong they do. Love is not supposed to delight in evilness but instead is to rejoice with the truth. But from where I am positioned, men delight themselves in evilness, and because I have exposed the truth, I have now become my husband's enemy. I was taught that love always protects, always trusts, always hopes, always perseveres—but now, when I wake, I find that the sweetness of what I was taught has manifested itself as a nightmare.

It was a long ride home from church and an even longer week. I had finally released the one thing that had boiled over from my mind into my spirit until it had grown into ownership of my very being. I had released it, and it was ugly, but the release had brought some peace to my soul because it had swollen up inside me so much that it had become hard for me to carry. I had to let it out or die. Now all that Gabriel and I shared was hours and then days of silence—a silence hung so heavily in the air that I felt as if I would suffocate. Our days were filled with too many moments of not trying to look at each other. The eyes reveal so much about the spirit.

Later that week, Gabriel was summoned by Reverend Parkinson for a meeting at the church with the other men. Lord only knows what was said and what conclusions they came to. Gabriel never spoke about it, and I did not have the strength to ask. But now that I think about it, the most ironic thing about the whole matter was that years later, Reverend Parkinson, his wife, and two of their female slaves all died from the same disease. Little did I know that when I had that outburst in church, I was

56

exposing the pastor's sin because Reverend Parkinson was just as guilty as Gabriel.

The following week, Daisy, my sister in-law, came to see me. Daisy was married to Gabriel's older brother, Jed, who had been deceased for about five years. It was said that he died at the hand of a slave trying to escape from the plantation. His grandfather had walked up just as Jed was being killed and he avenged his grandson's death by killing the slave. This dreadful situation left Daisy to live the life of a young widow. Daisy was such a beautiful woman—tall and thin with naturally curly blonde hair. When you saw her smile, you knew that you had experienced God's peace. But there was such hardness in her eyes—hardness that seemed so out of place among her delicate beauty, beauty so graceful, like a freshly painted portrait. Other men did desire her, but she was not to be bothered. And so I assumed that the love she had shared with Jed was so strong and complete that she did not desire another to take his place. She was not a lonesome widow. She made it known that she was content in her singleness. They had had no children, and she kept herself busy by being God's helping hand for others in need.

When she arrived that sunny afternoon, I was sitting on the porch trying to crochet some sense into what my life had come to be. Daisy had such sweetness about her that she gave you the freedom of speaking what was in your heart and knowing it was safe. So as she walked up the steps and approached me, I began to cry. She dried my tears with one of her white gloves as she comforted me.

"There, there, Margaret, just let it all out so you can feel better."

I began to ask my questions as if she had the answers. "Who told that lie on me, Daisy? Who said I was not woman enough to handle my man in bed? Who planted that ugly seed in Gabriel's mind? They told him that Margaret could never endure all the passion he had and desired to give a woman—that it would be so cruel of him to seek such beastly pleasure from me, a white woman. Why do they think that we are just like flowers made mostly to look at, to admire, but not to touch? We don't crumble when they touch us. We don't. Am I perceiving this right? Daisy, who did this cruel thing to me, to you, and to all white women?"

"It doesn't matter who," Daisy replied. "What matters is that the men believe it, and so the women have learned to endure the pain of it. Talkin' to me like this is all right, but Margaret, you can't keep goin' around havin' this conversation with others. Even though their hearts are familiar with this pain, politically they will not allow their lips to speak it. You are going to cause more harm than good for you and Gabriel. You don't want the two of you to be treated as outcasts and disrespected in this community. Would you have everythin' that Gabriel and his family have worked so hard to build be destroyed over somethin' that you, bein' a woman, have no control over?" Daisy could always speak that straightforward truth that would bring my mind to a sobering position.

"Was Jed the same way with you? Are all of them doing the same thing? Are there no exceptions?" I asked.

She held her breath for a moment. "No, my darling, Jed was much worse than that," She said in a harsh, unfamiliar voice.

"How could anyone be worse than that?" I asked.

After a long moment of silence, she said, "Jed was intimate with men." At that moment, it was as if someone or something had sucked all the air out of my surroundings. I could not believe what my ears had heard. And it felt as if my heart was bleeding for Daisy—sweet, sweet Daisy, so loving, so caring, and so beautiful. Now I understood the hardness of her eyes.

She told me how one night she had gone to the barn with plans of surprising Jed with hopes of getting him to make wild, passionate love with her right there, just as they had done in the beginning of their marriage. But instead, she found that he had bound one of the young boy slaves and was forcing himself on him. She was so devastated that she ran back to the house. The shock of it left her speechless. Her husband, who had always been passionate with her, was able to do this thing. The next morning, the slave was found dead. She could not bring herself to speak of this to anyone, and so what she knew had made her sick for days in bed.

Remembering that she had once overheard Jed's grandfather questioning him as to why, when he was sent to purchase slaves, a young boy slave always died or escaped. She went on to say that on the night Jed was killed, she had heard a gunshot and then, seconds later, another. She believed that on the night when he was killed, his grandfather had found him in the act, just as she had, and killed his grandson in anger and humiliation—and then killed the slave to make it seem one way when it was another. That was why she desired to just stay single. She was locked inside herself, never able to trust another man.

I realized then that though we look at people and assume their lives are one way, we never really know what life has presented to them.

BITTERNESS/SWEETNESS

At that moment, I stopped talking to Someday, glancing around to make sure no one was in hearing distance because others had come to the lake to fish. Once assured, I continued where I had left off.

Well, time went on, and nothing really changed regarding this matter. However, the pain we shared kept Miss Sister and me close to each other. Gabriel continued to pleasure himself with me when he desired to do so and do the same with Miss Sister. The sad part about it was that I never turned him down. I was always hungry for his touch, for his body. This ugliness was passed down from white man to white man, generation after generation, and had become the natural thing for them to do—and for us, the white women, to accept. They saw no reason to consider how it damaged the women. The white man did what the white man wanted to do at the expense of everyone else.

Well, as time passed, things got better, and the ladies at the church began inviting me to their different gatherings. This encouraged me to extend invitations to them to my home, and they accepted. I guess this was their Christian way of showing their forgiveness to me for revealing the demon that held their spirits captive. No matter how disgusting, no matter how hard, and no matter how ruthless, it was the truth. Sometimes the truth is so fearful that we would rather be allies of darkness. Come to think of it, not one of them ever spoke of it in my presence, even though surely in secret times some gossip did take place.

Anyway, during these gatherings, it was as if my outburst had never happened. But Lord, we knew it did. I guess being the fine, upstanding, white Christian women we were somehow made us decide that we could sweep anything under the rug if we came together, dressed in the fineness of life, and drank tea in the homes where we displayed the richness of our worldly goods. The Good Book says, [Mark 8:36] "What does it profit a man to gain the world and lose his soul?" For truly our minds, our wills and our emotions were lost in the wrappings of tainted sin. We all knew it existed and we knew it so well, but we chose to turn our heads as if we had no power.

Just when I thought that things were finally getting better and that all that could go wrong had gone wrong, guess what? Things got worse! One day, while serving some hot English tea for some lady friends and me, Miss Sister fainted right there in the middle of the parlor. Thank the Lord that no one got burned by the tea. But the shock came when I found out later that she was with child. There was no reason to ask by whom because I knew the answer to that.

That night, I cried so much that I knew God's ears had to be aching. "Why has this happened to me, Lord? Of all the people in my world, why Miss Sister? She is the one I grew up with, my saving angel who always kept Mama and Papa from finding out about those foolish and wild crazy things I did. Why her, Lord?" I prayed.

Why had life made her become the source of my hatred—a hatred so strong that it filled my bones with bitterness? Even though I had remained merciful towards her in light of our situation, still it seemed that that wasn't enough. And now this! How was I to survive this?

"I just want to hate her, Lord! I just want to hate her! But deep down, I love her because she has been my one true friend. Lord, you said that a friend will lay down their life for another. Miss Sister has done that for me. God, I can't tell anyone but you about this. If anyone knew that I, Margaret, a fine, upstanding white woman, looked upon a slave as her friend, surely I would be an outcast amongst society. I would bring much shame and disgrace to my Gabriel, my mama and papa—why, the whole family would never be able to live it down."

As I pondered the unfairness of life, the whole room seemed to spin around in my head. In my heart, I felt one way, but the world would have me pretend it to be another. The world was all right with Gabriel sleeping with a slave gal, but this same world would persecute me for calling her friend.

I could not allow her to work in my house as her belly swelled into motherhood. I would be constantly reminded that she had been able to conceive by Gabriel, and I, his wife, could not. Miss Sister was not happy about her present state. She kept saying that she was going to make it right. How could she think that she could ever make this right? Often I wondered what kind of conversation transpired between the two of them. Did Gabriel ever ask how she felt? Did he rub her stomach? Was he happy even though the child was not going to be white? Now that she was carrying his child, would she think kindly about him? And she said that she was going to make it right!

Rosa Lee was the fifteen-year-old slave Gabriel chose to work in the house, doing the chores Miss Sister had done. Before, Rosa Lee had been the wash girl, washing the clothes, bed sheets, and such, but now Miss Sister was doing that. Then, as I hadn't had enough to handle, about four months later, I became sick and was in bed. Rosa Lee, God bless her soul, was there doing all she could to make me feel better, but nothing helped, and so Gabriel sent for the doctor. I was fearful, not knowing what was wrong, but after the examination, the doctor announced that I was pregnant. I guess God decided that I was long overdue for some joy in my life, and my being pregnant did bring us much joy.

I never could have imagined that my being in the motherly way would add so much excitement to Gabriel's life. But he began to smile more and would laugh at the silliest things. This man I married changed right before my eyes, so swiftly becoming attentive, patient, and caring, always wanting to make sure I had everything I needed. I noticed that he would sometimes just stand and look at me with great satisfaction and admiration. Once again, I felt special and loved by Gabriel. But even with that, I still wished that things were good between Miss Sister and me. How I missed those times when things were good between us. I wished I could share this news with her. Life could be funny that way—she was carrying my husband's baby and yet I wished for her to take part in my joy.

Gabriel sent word to our folks back home, and both our mothers decided that they would plan to come when it was close to the arrival of the baby. The grandpapas made it be known that they were hoping for a boy to carry on the Butler blood line, and Gabriel wasted no time in choosing a boy's name for the baby: Paul Andrew Butler—Paul after his father, and Andrew after Papa.

I told him, "You don't know. It could be a girl."

But with that big, silly grin on his face, he did not hesitate in replying, "I have faith in God, Margaret, that it will be a son, and you and no one else will get me to thinkin' otherwise. Trust me—there is no need for a girl's name."

"I may want a Margaret Ann," I said jokingly.

"No need for a girl's name," he repeated.

"But don't you think Jenny Butler would be a good name for a girl?"

"Again, I say to you, Mrs. Margaret Butler, there is no need for a girl's name," he said, smiling down at me. Then, suddenly, he pulled me close and kissed me. Still holding me, he said, "You are carrying my son, my heir, and the heir of your father and my father. It is a boy!"

12

MAKING THINGS RIGHT

I stood up and led Someday away from the lake, suddenly fearful of sharing what was on my mind.

Everything was going well until one particular morning. I woke up with the feeling of such uneasiness in the air. A few moments later, the quiet of the house was broken by the sound of something tumbling down the steps. Despite my delicate condition, I ran from the bedroom to the top of the staircase and saw Miss Sister lying at the bottom of the stairs. I screamed so loud that I am sure Lucifer himself became scared. I rushed down the stairs, crying, "Miss Sister! Miss Sister!" Finally, I reached her, and though I don't remember how, I found myself sitting on the foyer floor with Miss Sister's head in my lap.

In the midst of my crying, she looked up at me, and the only thing she said was "I told you I would make it right." And then she closed her eyes.

I had not known she was even in the house. Next thing I remember was Rosa Lee yelling for Luther, the house boy, to go and get Belle, an old slave woman. Not only was she the midwife, but she did all the doctoring for the slaves as well. She was a tall, big-boned woman with white hair on jet-black skin. All the slaves swore she had strong, healing hands. Once she arrived, Rosa Lee helped me back upstairs so I would not see them move Miss Sister. I told Rosa Lee to make sure that Belle came to see me once she finished seeing about Miss Sister.

Rosa Lee thought I would never stop crying, but she finally managed to get me to calm down and get back in bed. It seemed to take forever for Belle to come to see me.

"Ms. Margaret, I never saw so much blood in all my life. The baby did not survive the fall, and we almost lost that gal," Belle said.

"Is she going to be all right, Belle?" I asked.

"I reckon she will, ma'am, but right now we's got to keep a close watch on her."

"And the baby?" I asked.

"It was a little gal baby. I had Luther bury it in back of Miss Sister's house," Belle said.

It was a frightful time, 'cause for days, Miss Sister was sweating and talking out of her head like something crazy, just rambling on and on. "Can't marry Simon … no babies for Simon, no babies for nobody … Devil's baby in my belly … Get it out, get it out! Get the Devil's baby out my belly!"

She carried on for two days like this, and during the day, no one could pry me away from Miss Sister's bedside. I was right there when she opened her eyes. Her eyes were so different, displaying the cold hardness of a spirit encased in pain.

"Lord, Miss Sister, I am so glad to see you open your eyes."

"The baby, the baby," she said, her hands searching her stomach.

Before I could force an answer, she whispered, "I told you I would make it right," looking at me from an unknown, faraway place. "Now your child will be Master Gabriel's firstborn."

"Hush, Miss Sister. Don't talk so. I did not know you were in the house. Child, you could have killed yourself."

She answered, "Make no matter, Miss Margaret. I's already the livin' dead."

Belle said that due to the amount of damage done to Miss Sister's body, she would likely never conceive again. But Miss Sister just smiled and said it was God's way of blessing and protecting her. During this time, I made sure that Miss Sister was well taken care of, and when she was back on her feet, I had her back working in the house, and Rosa Lee went back to her old chores.

By this time, I suspected that Gabriel was doing his business with Rosa Lee. I guess some things never change. I was pregnant, and surely if he thought I could not handle being intimate with him before my present state, then now, as a pregnant white woman, I was too fragile even for touching. And Miss Sister, to him, was damaged goods. Hell, he talked about her as if she was some horse he owned. But later, Miss Sister heard that on some occasions, Rosa Lee had taken chicken blood and planted it in her bed to keep Gabriel from fooling with her. When Miss Sister told me about it, we laughed until tears came out of our eyes. Why, we were laughing so hard and loud that we forgot that Gabriel was in the house. He wanted to know what was going on, and you know that really made it funnier, so funny we almost died laughing. Why, I could imagine Rosa Lee wringing the neck of that chicken, draining the blood in a jar, and fixing it to look like it was her blood when she heard Gabriel coming. But even though the laughter was welcome, as we looked at each other, we realized that it still did not end the life of the pain that seemed to take such joy in residing in our hearts.

Time had brought me into the seventh month of my pregnancy, and the anticipation of the birth had knit Miss Sister and me back together. Why, it seemed as if we were closer than we were before the nightmares of life had begun to surface. It was as if the baby had two mothers waiting for it to arrive. Even though

I was scared, I still felt safe knowing that Miss Sister would be there with me.

The joy had made us become one as we looked forward to and prepared for that special moment. I made sure that Miss Sister went with me when it was time to do shopping for the baby. Those times reminded me of when we were little girls captivated by the different things that filled the store shelves and counters. It made you want to buy every pretty thing in sight.

Luther was the best carpenter, and Gabriel had him make the baby a crib. The women's crocheting and quilting group made all sorts of beautiful gifts for the baby. Truly, it was a special time, even though as the delivery approached and I got bigger, it sometimes did not feel like it. Comfort and sleep became strangers to me in the last month. Why, I did not remember when last I could look down and see my feet.

Gabriel was so loving during this time. He would often rub my stomach and lay his head there as he talked to the baby, but best of all was when he would rub my feet. It was so comforting and soothing to my whole body. I really felt like hibernating because I was real ugly at this stage, but Gabriel would often try to assure me that I was so beautiful. What really shocked me about him was that at times he would bathe me. To make the baths more special, he would surprise me with scented oils and soaps he had purchased. The first time, I cried because it was so endearing to see my husband in such a compassionate state. He wiped my tears and then kissed my lips ever so gently.

As the baby's kicks became stronger, Gabriel grew more confident that it had to be a boy. Having a boy would be so special for both families, but my only requirement for this baby was for it to be healthy. Now that was my main concern—ten fingers, ten toes, two eyes, one mouth, and one nose. That would make me one happy mother.

13

TWO MOTHERS

Someday and I reached the well. Zachariah was drawing water and offered me a drink. I accepted and made sure that Someday was given some as well before we continued our walk.

The anticipation of the coming of the baby was so great that our parents could not bear to wait until after the birth to come. After all, this was not just the birth of a grandchild—this was the birth of the first grandchild on both sides of the family, the first extension. They came, and with the exception of my growing discomfort as the time drew near, the excitement in the house reminded me of when I was a child waiting for Christmas to come. Our mothers brought not only their personal gifts, but also gifts that had been sent by family and friends from back home.

Even in the midst of such joy, sadness still found its way to me. Miss Sister found out from Homer, the carriage driver, that Simon had passed on. Homer said that he had died in his sleep with a smile on his face, and it had surprised everybody because he had not been sick. But what was most shocking about the news was that it happened on the same day Miss Sister fell down the stairs. Miss Sister said that now she knew that Simon would always be in her spirit.

Both our mothers made sure I was comfortable, and Miss Sister made sure I had whatever I wanted to eat. Mrs. Butler, being such a remarkable pianist, would often play beautiful music for me while Mama brushed my hair or rubbed my feet. I was in much need of all this attention. And believe you me—I did enjoy it.

Miss Sister shared in the joy of preparing the baby's room, making sure that all the items they brought were put in their proper places. She and I folded the baby clothing together as we tried to imagine what he or she would look like in the tiny clothes. Would the baby have my eyes, or Gabriel's ears? What was it going to be like, bathing and dressing such a tiny one? The softness of their skin, the sound of their crying, and watching them drift into a peaceful sleep ...

One day, Daisy paid us a surprise visit, and Mr. and Mrs. Butler were overjoyed because it had been awhile since they had seen her. Immediately they made her promise to visit them soon. They were always pleased in having her for a daughter-in-law. Even though Jed was gone, their love for Daisy had survived. Mama and Papa were very happy as well to see her again, having last seen her at our wedding. I assured them that Daisy and I had grown to be dear to one another, and Daisy agreed.

On that day, Daisy came with one of the most endearing gifts—a hand-carved rocking chair. She said that all new mothers needed a rocking chair for spending many hours bonding with the baby. The chair was a very important item because it would be used to rock in while reading and singing to the baby, for consoling the baby when it did not feel well, and for putting it to sleep.

"Daisy, where did you find such a beautiful chair?" I asked. "The work is breathtaking."

With such a distance in her voice, she answered, "Jed had it made for me. He hoped that we would one day have children of our own." Then she gave me a look as if to say, "Thank God that did not happen," and with a quickness, she added, "Now, Margaret, I did not come here to talk about me. This is to be the happiest occasion for you, my dear." Then she gave me a hug.

Daisy's visit was such a blessing, and we could not wait to show her the baby's room. She thought it was so sweet, and the rocking chair made it even more special.

"I am goin' to be Aunt Daisy!" she said with so much joy, as if this was the first time the thought had entered her mind.

And I said, "Yes, and aunts are very special people. They get many, many hugs and kisses for the rest of their lives."

We all laughed. Later we realized that we ladies had just chatted the day away.

We convinced Daisy to stay for dinner by bribing her with her favorite food: smothered pork chops. At dinner, the men allowed the women to do most of the talking while they did most of the eating. Mama and Mrs. Butler had much to tell us about things happening back home. They mentioned that Mr. Murray's barn had burned and that some of the horses died in the fire, but the townspeople had come together and helped them rebuild it. Papa commented on how that was, indeed, a powerful display of Christian love and that Pastor Forkner preached about it the following Sunday morning.

Mrs. Butler went on to tell us that Jake Beavers could not get any of the town's women to marry him after Rebecca died, leaving him with six children. So, after a year of him writing letters to churches and publishing personal advertisements in magazines and newspapers, he got himself a mail-order bride. They courted by writing each other letters, and of course, she sent him a photograph. It turned out that she was a widow with one child of her own. He needed a mama for those children, and she needed a father for her nine-year-old daughter, as well as financial stability. Mrs. Butler said that she seemed to be such a sweetheart and that Jake and the children were glad to have them as part of their family. Of course, making the adjustment was a little rough, but surely that was to be expected. Her name was Anna Bell, and her daughter was Cassy. It turned out that both our parents had had them as dinner guests in their homes.

I inquired about how our friends Edward and Laura were doing and was told what a fine doctor Edward was and how blessed the town was to have him. Laura had helped tremendously in raising money for the hospital by sponsoring a ball and inviting all the town's wealthy people.

"Those two are a perfect match for each other," Mrs. Butler said.

I said, "If I had not been expectin' the baby, Gabriel and I would have been right there dancin' in the midst of all those fine people. Why, I just love dressin' up for a gala occasion, enjoyin' the rich foods, drinkin' the best wines, and havin' those informative conversations. Mama, I think I am goin' to write them a letter, and we will get a nice gift for y'all to carry back to Edward and Laura. How I miss our dear friends! Maybe after the baby comes, we will pay them a visit. Even better—I would love to have the two of them to come visit us."

"But their loss is truly my gain," Daisy said, going on to share how happy she was to have me here close to her. Mama agreed that nothing could take the place of being around family, and with her being so far away, knowing that I had someone like Daisy close by would help her not to worry as much.

Everything was going well that night until Mama mentioned that it was truly a blessing that Miss Sister, still having milk, would be able to serve as a wet nurse for the baby.

"No, she will not!" I screamed. "I am goin' to breastfeed my own baby!"

"But Margaret, you don't understand how painful and messy that can be," Mama said.

"Now, sugar, please listen to your mama," said Mrs. Butler. "You do not understand how hard this will be for you. We older women know and do not want you to have to experience that."

"No disrespect to you, Mrs. Butler, or to you, Mama, but breastfeedin' my baby will be a special way for us to bond. I have often imagined what it will be like holdin' the baby close while nursing. God provides the milk, and I will proudly breastfeed my baby. Miss Sister is no more a woman than I am. If she can endure the mess and the pain of it, then surely I can. I will breastfeed, and that is the end of this conversation," I said, excusing myself for bed.

I was still furious with them when Miss Sister came in to help me dress for bed. I said to her, "Why, Miss Sister, it is not enough that they told me I would not enjoy being intimate with my husband—and then made him believe that I, a white woman, was too delicate for his intimate passions. Things are the way they are because of their lies. Now Mama and Mrs. Butler are saying that I could not handle breastfeedin' my own baby; but instead you should have that responsibility."

"And just what did you say to that, Miss Margaret?" Miss Sister asked.

"God provides the milk, and I will proudly breastfeed my baby," I replied.

Then Miss Sister stepped close to me and, holding my gaze, she whispered, "And you will breastfeed your baby."

Another day went by before finally the baby decided that it was time to meet the world. The only ones in this arena were the midwife, Miss Sister, and me. With each pain, I felt a hatred for Gabriel because he had gotten to sit back and wait while my body grew out of proportion, to sleep while sleeplessness and discomfort resided with me. And now, in the final moments, I had to do all the suffering. Each time I screamed, it seemed to be with a force so strong that the walls of the room would burst at the seams. I was so tired of pushing and being told not to push and then to push again. I wondered why the baby wouldn't just pop out like the muscadine.

After much pushing and screaming, the long-awaited moment came, and I was introduced to Paul Andrew Butler. Gabriel and I had fulfilled our duty by birthing a male child. Paul Andrew Butler—such a heavy name for one so tiny to carry. But not only was he to bear the responsibility of the name, he was also to bear the hope, the bloodline, and the vision for the present and future generations.

In that moment, as my eyes beheld this tiny little miracle, I realized that all the pain and anguish I had experienced trying to get him here were traded for the joy and peace of God. This was a different level of love—a love that could not be bought, a love that kindled hope and faith for the better things from life, a love that was pure and would be unconditionally given. This was a mother's love.

When I held him for the first time, I felt a fulfillment that I had not known existed. I thought to myself, *So much warmth coming from this little person.* It was at that moment that I touched him on his tiny nose and called him Andy.

"Your name is Paul Andrew Butler, but to your mama, you will always be Andy," I said, looking down and smiling at him. I had never dreamed that God would allow something so special to come from me. Now my life had purpose, and I knew that I could never tire of looking at little Andy. I imagined that this was what the baby angels looked like in heaven—such sweetness to kiss, the sweetness producing lullabies from my heart. And with the lullabies, I would often find myself singing God's praises over little Andy, sending him into a state of calmness and then sleep.

When Gabriel entered the room, I knew without words being spoken that his heart was blessed. He kissed me gently on my forehead and said, "Margaret, you have given me my heart's desire. Having a son has stretched the Butler bloodline to another generation. Not only have I lived to see this day, but most importantly, my father has also lived to witness the birth of Paul Andrew Butler, and knows that now his bloodline flows even further. I could never love you enough for giving me a healthy son—my son."

At that time, Papa tapped at the door, and our parents came in. And I do believe that the sunshine entered the room with them. That was how bright the smiles were on their faces. My mama was so proud of my bringing this little angel into our lives.

"Margaret, now you will understand why I am the way I am when it comes to you, my darlin' daughter. You have changed our lives forever. Now you are Mother and I am Grandmother."

"Darlin', you have done well, and truly we have been blessed to be grandparents of this fine baby boy," Mrs. Butler said, drying her eyes.

"Well, Andrew, now we old fellows got more to live for," Judge Butler said.

"And much to celebrate!" Papa said.

Then I said, "Yes, and the other thing I want everybody to understand is that I hope I never have to go through this ordeal again. God, I pray, Mama, that I will be like you."

Mama interrupted, "Oh Lord, and what do you mean by that, Margaret?"

"Just that I hope I never have any more children. How do women just keep havin' babies? Mrs. Butler, I bet you were scared when you found out that you were pregnant with Gabriel." Mrs. Butler just laughed. Then the men left the room.

But I continued, "If carryin' the child is not enough, the stomach stretchin' from here to there, and becomin' a stranger to your own feet—well, you just don't look normal. Then come the pains, and they make you feel as if there is a war going on inside your belly that will kill you before you can birth the baby into this world. Then the baby comes by stretching your butt open until it is almost big enough to put the whole town in it."

"Margaret, hush! Child, you can speak so foolish at times," Mama said.

"Mrs. Butler, will my butt ever go back to the size it was before this? Please tell me it will," I begged.

I could tell that I was not handling this well because both our mothers were uncomfortable. Still, I continued, "I am so glad that God decided to make everybody happy by givin' us a son because I declare, Mama, that I am about to go crazy just thinkin' right now about this ever happenin' to me again. I believe that this is the only thing that could make me fearful of bein' intimate with my Gabriel. And that is sayin' a lot. Truly, to give birth is to experience hell, and the only thing that brought heaven to me was when I laid my eyes on little Andy."

"Ah, Margaret, that sounds so sweet—*little Andy*," Mama said, smiling.

"Mrs. Butler, who do you think he looks like?" I asked.

"Why, child, when you see Gabriel's baby picture, you see your own son. With those long fingers and arms, no doubt he will be tall just like his daddy," she said in such a prideful way.

"Well, he has Gabriel's nose and ears, but his mouth is definitely just like yours, Margaret," Mama said, as if she had to make sure that everyone knew that her child deserved some of the credit for how little Andy looked.

It was amazing how our lives changed for the better after having little Andy. In spite of all the madness life had presented to Miss Sister and me, little Andy brought joy for us to share— because sharing him was what we did. It was as if he had two mamas. Miss Sister was right there encouraging me as I fulfilled my responsibility of breastfeeding him. I was so awkward at doing it; and besides that, I hated my breast going back and forth from being hard like a rock, and then the milk would run like a river, making a mess of my clothes. I was able to endure it all because Miss Sister was always waiting and willing to help in any way that she could.

Miss Sister would walk little Andy during those sleepless nights when he had colic, and when he was teething, she did whatever she could to help ease that baby's gums. Miss Sister would not allow Rosa to even wash his clothes. She said that the baby's clothes needed special care, and so she did the washing. Then we discovered that finally life had blessed us with its beauty and another side of love. This was a love that brought the life back into those big beautiful eyes of Miss Sister's and joy back into my heart.

It was really something when he started to make sounds and most exciting when we realized that he was trying for the first time to say *Daddy* and, later on, *Mama*. Miss Sister and I were tickled to death when he would do his best to say *Miss Sister*. Finally, when little Andy learned to walk, it was music to our ears listening to the patter of his tiny feet. And if you turned your head just for a second, he would get into something so quickly. As he got older, he enjoyed hiding, and he was good at it. But it would tickle him so when we did find him. He would laugh so loud, just like a big boy. Truly, he was more than a handful.

Little Andy always enjoyed the church singing; he would clap his hands and try to sing with the choir. Everybody knew that Brother Thompson was going to shout before the church service was over, and one particular Sunday, little Andy surprised us all by jumping to his feet and trying to shout just like him. Little Andy was just stomping, kicking, and clapping all off beat when all of a sudden, he raised both his hands up and ran down the center aisle of the church. Seeing him doing that was so funny, everybody had to laugh—and it was a long time before they stopped talking about it.

It was also pleasing to see Gabriel bonding with his son. He would always make time to play with little Andy, and on other occasions, he would take Andy for walks and rides, leaving me behind. I remember the first time he rode a horse with little Andy. It scared me so much, but I was amazed at how little Andy seemed to enjoy himself. I came to realize that he was just like his mama was as a child: not afraid of anything. When little Andy was able to ride on his own, Gabriel gave him a pony, and little Andy named him Star.

It became tradition for us to take little Andy back home every year for Christmas so those times could be shared with his grandparents, and they, in turn, would always make his birthdays special by coming and giving a huge celebration. Miss Sister always prided herself in baking the birthday cake. Going home for Christmas always served as a twofold blessing because it allowed Gabriel and me to visit with Edward and Laura. Edward and Laura still had no children of their own, but they always made sure that they spent time with little Andy when we were there for our visits. They felt as if they were his honorary aunt and uncle.

Little Andy proved to be a fast learner in his school studies. He never shied away from anything or anybody. He would carry on a conversation like an old man. At times I would act as if I did not know something just to have my little old man think that he was teaching his mama. He was always eager to see if he could do and try new things. Why, it was so amazing to see how fast Gabriel taught him to ride a horse with such confidence! He also would allow little Andy to help feed and brush the horses.

Miss Sister, not wanting to be outdone, was determined to teach him how to be an excellent fisherman. I could never forget Miss Sister and him wearing their two-of-a-kind fishing hats as we walked to the pond. While walking, we would often sing, and sometimes Miss Sister would make up songs. It didn't matter, because little Andy loved to sing. I went along because I found it to be so much fun just watching Miss Sister while she was teaching little Andy. They would dig for worms, and after watching Miss Sister handle them for the first time, little Andy would pick them up without a second thought. But sometimes he wanted to give the worms a name. Now that was really different. In the beginning, Miss Sister had a way of tricking little Andy into thinking he had baited the fishing hook all on his own by making a big fuss over it. We would carry a basket of food, and

I would sit and knit while they fished, just making a day of it. Sometimes, while waiting for the fish to bite, I would tell him a story to help pass the time.

With him not being afraid of anything, we knew that great things were to be expected for his life. That boy was the joy of the household because he was always playing jokes on Miss Sister and me—he always kept us laughing about something. But he knew to remain calm when dealing with his Daddy.

14

LITTLE ANDY BECOMES ANDREW

Then Someday and I found ourselves coming out of the barn after looking around. As we continued our walk, I remembered that I had been sharing about my son.

When little Andy turned eight years old, our parents came to visit as they always did, but this was not to be the usual birthday celebration visit. Our fathers wanted to talk with Gabriel regarding sending little Andy away to boarding school. They wanted to send him to High Point, the same school that Gabriel, his father, and grandfather had attended. I knew it was their family tradition, but for some reason I did not see it coming. I was so devastated that I thought my heart was going to stop beating. I could not imagine what my life would be like without little Andy underfoot. They seemed to not understand that he was my joy and my child. I was his mother, and the thought of them sending him away was merely ripping my heart out. Instead, they kept talking about the quality of the school and how there would be a number of senior teachers appointed as housemasters, along with advisors that would watch over the students at all times, particularly outside of school hours. Also, in each dorm was a matron, a house tutor, and a housekeeper. Still, his mother would not be there. I did all

I could to make sure this decision was not easy for either one of them.

Gabriel tried to reason with me by pointing out that we would visit from time to time and little Andy would be home for the holidays. But the holidays would not make up for his spending what was left of his childhood and the majority of his adolescent life away from his family. I was going to miss the upcoming years of those changing times in my son's life. But I was just a woman, and my opinion did not matter.

The men made all the arrangements, and that following fall, little Andy left me and Miss Sister, and so did the joy of the house. Those sleepless nights without him tortured my soul. I could do nothing but pray and cry, wondering if my baby felt afraid and abandoned in his new surroundings. I found no comfort in my husband because Gabriel took it all to be woman's foolishness, which was what I had expected of him. My son could have grown to be a man without leaving his family.

Fall was always a joyous season because we were looking forward to traveling home for our long visit of Thanksgiving, Christmas, and New Year's, but with Little Andy leaving for school, that time was most unbearable, even though he would be home for the holidays. It was as if someone had died. At first I took to staying in bed with the curtains drawn tight so the darkness would not escape the room. My need to nurture the sadness made the sun my enemy, and anger was the prisoner of my soul. As if that wasn't enough, out of nowhere, Gabriel's cousin Bunny and her husband, Matthew Bentley, paid us a surprise visit. They were traveling farther south to meet up with friends for some business endeavor and had decided to stop along the way and pay us a short visit.

Marriage had not calmed her down, for she was still a big flirt. It appeared she had married the right man because they were two of a kind. They drank heavily each night—even had Gabriel acting foolish with them. Even though I hated having them in our home, I still was very hospitable toward them. After all, they were my husband's relatives. On the morning they were leaving, I was so happy, knowing that soon they would be long gone—but Satan quickly took over. We were all at the table finishing breakfast and, I hoped, the last of our pleasantries when I stepped away and suddenly heard a loud outburst. Immediately I returned to find Bunny yelling at Miss Sister.

"You dropped that knife on purpose! You wanted to cut my hand!" Then Bunny slapped her.

"No, ma'am," Miss Sister started, trying to explain.

But before she could say another word, Matthew replied, "Nigger, you callin' my wife a liar? Gabriel, what you gonna do about this? This here nigger gal tried to cut my wife and has the nerve to call her a liar. Now she has gone too far. She needs to be whipped. Tell me, what you gon' do about this matter? Who rules your house—you, or the niggers?"

"Gabriel!" I screamed.

Quickly he responded, "Don't you say a word, Margaret, because if you do, you will force me to sell her off, and that right there would be goin' against the promise I made to your mama and papa. Don't you try me this day."

Since his manhood was threatened, I knew he would do just that, so keepin' my mouth shut was the only way I could protect Miss Sister. Next thing I knew, Gabriel had dragged Miss Sister out of the house and had her beat by the overseer. Matthew and Bonny left immediately afterward as if they had just come for the purpose of causing hell in my home. In all those years, Miss Sister had escaped being whipped. Now the thought of strawberries was not so funny anymore.

During this time, there really wasn't much joy to share with Gabriel. We even saw no need to continue to share the same bedroom. I truly believe that I would have died from a broken heart if not been for the hope of seeing little Andy during his brief visits home. But just as I had survived the past disappointments of life, eventually I pressed my way, and Miss Sister and I made the necessary adjustments for this as well.

It was worse when I thought about how our fathers had come and aided in taking my son away, disrupting my life, and then returned home to life as usual. Gabriel did the same. As time went by, I kept myself busy with church gatherings and my women society groups. But always, my heart was geared toward visiting little Andy and having him home for holidays. The irony of that was that during his visits, I had to share him with our folks because we were always with them for the holidays—just no winning for me.

Finally, the years passed, little Andy became Andrew, and I found myself having to reach up just to give him a hug. Sometimes, when he was in those silly moods, he would pick me up and swing me around. At those times, I would think about how amazing life is. It seemed like just yesterday Andrew was a tiny baby in my arms, and now he had arms strong enough to pick me up.

Something changed with Andrew when he was around twelve years old. You know how it is when you recognize that something is different, but you just can't put your finger on it? But later I found out what it was—or rather, Miss Sister found out and told me. It seemed that Gabriel had made one of the slave women sleep with our son. It was said that he chose a full-grown woman so she could teach him the proper way to have intercourse, and if that wasn't enough, Gabriel watched them. I guess this was something else that the men prided themselves in doing. This was yet another thing to add to the frustration of the women—because there was nothing we could do about it.

The years kept coming and going, but still, we always looked forward to visiting our parents for the holidays. Shopping, decorating, eating the festive foods, and attending the dances made the holidays joyful. Of course, we can't forget about the men's excitement over deer hunting. They even taught Andrew how to shoot, and he killed a deer his first time hunting with them. Gabriel and both grandfathers were so proud of Andrew. The head was mounted over the fireplace in the judge's study.

Later, as Andrew became older, he would travel on his own and meet us at our parents'. Sometimes he would bring a friend from school to share the holidays with us. If it made Andrew happy, then all was well with me. Those were special times and the only sweetness for my soul. It was the life source of my existence. Nothing else really mattered.

Then the day came when I looked up and found my son to truly be a man. If anyone were to ask me why I noticed or what had happened to make me see the change, I could not have explained it, but what I could say was that at that moment, I thought to myself, *Where did the time go?* It seemed unreal that I had once held him in my arms, doing all I could to make him feel secure in the uncertainty of this world. But the world proved not to be the enemy; the enemy was the men in my life. Because of them and their having the authority to make the decisions regarding our lives, my son had grown up away from home without the everyday joy of the presence of his mother. Instead, most of his days were shared with strangers, and because of that, they knew more about my son than I did.

Finally, the day came when Andrew finished this phase of his schooling, and he graduated with top honors. Papa, Mama, the Butlers, Gabriel, and I were all there to witness and share in the glory of that moment in his life. Why, years later I could still close my eyes and hear them call his name and see him as he stepped forward—tall and handsome, his back straight—to shake hands and receive his diploma. Part of my excitement was in knowing that Andrew would be coming home. Miss Sister had traveled with us but was not allowed to attend the activities, but Andrew made sure that he visited with her while we were there.

Andrew being home was like a breath of fresh air. As always, he played jokes on Miss Sister and me, keeping us wondering what he would do next. We made sure he had all his favorite foods.

Often, he and Gabriel would go horseback riding. Miss Sister and I did get our fishing time in with him. As quickly as the breath of fresh air had come, it left because now it was time for Andrew to make a decision as to what career he wanted to pursue in life. The men gave him no opportunity to express himself, instead telling him what he was to become. So, thanks to Gabriel and both our fathers, Andrew studied law and completed his studies at Harvard University in Cambridge, Massachusetts. They had even decided that he would do his internship at the law firm of Miller and Ross, dear friends of his grandfather, Judge Butler. Everything went exactly the way they had planned it. This made the judge so proud that no one could have a conversation with him without him making Andrew's career the main topic. To him, it was very important for everyone to know that his grandson was following in the footsteps of his grandfather.

It was during his internship that Andrew met the lovely Agnes Ross, the daughter of Attorney Jeffery Ross, and she captivated his heart. After a lengthy time of being in her continuous company, he informed us of his feelings for her and invited us to come and meet her and her family. Andrew really wanted his father's approval before asking her father for her hand in marriage. We went, and I have to say that not only was she beautiful, but she also had a sweet spirit, with the personality of a well-groomed lady—but as I got to spend time with her, I could tell that if the situation presented itself, Agnes had no problem with being outspoken. Her mother commented about how she had shocked them by getting a shoulder-length haircut. But Agnes made it known that her haircut did not make her less of a woman. It put a smile on my face, and I knew then that I was going to enjoy getting to know her. She reminded me of myself at that age. Meeting her and her family was such a joy. It felt as if Gabriel and I had known them for years.

Being in Massachusetts was so refreshing; a change of scenery was exactly what I needed. During that time away from home,

Gabriel was the enchanting man I had married—very attentive, holding the doors open for me, kissing my hand, and when we danced, he would hold me close and, looking into my eyes like I was his only delight, he would smile and say sweet nothings to me. Oh, I played the game right along with him—the role of the lovely wife. I said all the smart and witty things and smiled at the right times. I was determined not to do anything that would embarrass our son.

Agnes and her mother, Helen, took me on a tour of all the fine shops, where I was able to purchase the latest in fashion. Gabriel told me to spare no expense, and I gladly took his advice—but then again, he never had any problems with my spending money. He always said that I represented him, and for that, he always wanted me to look my very best. I knew that I needed to take advantage of his wanting to show off because when we returned home, reality would surely set in, and Gabriel's attention would not belong to me. However, there was some joy in looking forward to returning home because some of the things I had purchased were to be worn to church. I could hardly wait to see the expressions on the ladies' lovely faces because there was no doubt that I would be the talk among them.

Helen and Jeffery made sure that we met the elite of their society by hosting a dinner in their luxurious home, and we dined at the most fabulous restaurants. Jeffery made it known that Andrew was doing an exceptional job as an intern and that he would be forever grateful to Judge Butler recommending him to their firm. Jeffery made it clear that he was not alone in this opinion, but that his partner, Fredrick Miller, and others of their firm felt the same. He went on to state that law was in Andrew's blood and that there was no doubt he had a prominent career ahead of him. Gabriel and I had such a wonderful time being there with Andrew that we hated to leave. But we both encouraged our son in the matter of asking for Agnes's hand in marriage. Not only was I happy at the thought of gaining Agnes as a daughter, but I was also pleased that Andrew would be marrying into a wonderful family—people who would love having him as part of their family. Before we left, we made Jeffery and Helen promise to come visit us.

Later, when Andrew came home for a visit, we were informed that Jeffery had given his blessing for Andrew to marry Agnes. Now Andrew's plan while home was to find the perfect engagement ring. He was going to propose when he returned to Cambridge. I saw this as an excellent opportunity to speak frankly with Andrew about the lies passed down from one generation to the next. Because of the men in the family, my son could not appreciate the conversation I had with him regarding the issue of whether to expect his wife to satisfy all his intimate needs.

"Your wife will be able to fulfill all your passionate desires. Do not believe the lies that have been passed down from generation to generation. It is demeaning for the white woman when her husband leaves her marriage bed to lay with the female slave." But because of the influence the men had over him, I had to hear these words from my son.

"Mother, I can't believe that we are having this conversation. Why, it is unbecoming and disrespectful for you as an upstanding white lady to talk so boldly about such private matters. These things should be discussed by men, but here you stand before me, talking as if you would know better than both my grandfathers, my father, and of course, the other men in this family. You are just one woman. What and who gives you the authority to speak for all white women?"

Before I knew it, I had slapped my beloved son and replied, "What did you say? I tell you, sir, the authority I have comes from all that I have endured because of the lies men have passed down—lies that were just accepted by the women because no one had the courage to tell the truth. I have suffered greatly and my sufferin' gives me the right to try and end this madness."

For the remainder of Andrew's visit, he avoided me, and he returned to Cambridge still upset. All I could do was pray about it. But later, we received the good news that Agnes had gladly accepted Andrew's proposal, and soon we found ourselves back in Massachusetts with our parents for the engagement party. When I set my eyes on my son, I knew that all was forgiven, and the hug he gave me confirmed what was in my spirit. Making our time there even more special was the arrival of Edward and Laura, who had been invited to share in this memorable occasion. This would truly be a joyous time in all our lives.

Of course Helen and Agnes made sure that Mama, Mrs. Butler, and Laura had the same experience of shopping at all the fine stores, just as I did on my first visit. The four of us found the most beautiful gowns for the party. And Jeffrey kept the men busy doing Lord knows what. One thing I knew was that Edward, being a doctor, wanted to visit the hospital there. Jeffery Ross contacted his good friend Dr. Thomas Sequel, and Edward was given a grand tour of the hospital. I thought that my engagement party had been something wonderful, but everything for this party was so eloquently done that it was breathtaking. The Rosses spared nothing, and what a wonderful celebration it was! Our parents and Edward and Laura enjoyed Massachusetts as much as Gabriel and I had on our first visit with the Ross family, and we all were looking forward to returning for the wedding.

Then came the day of hell on earth, and so quickly, all the goodness of life was gone again. During Andrew's internship, there was a fire at the office, and Andrew died trying to help someone else. For this I blamed the men of the family because it was their decision that had caused him to be there. My only child and their only grandchild! This tragedy made me so angry that bitterness ruled my heart. I prayed so hard for God to help me let go and forgive Gabriel and our fathers, the men making all the decisions, but the forgiveness just wouldn't come.

Everything that took place right after we found out about Andrew's death was lost in my mind. The only thing I could recall after that was waking up one day, screaming his name, even though I knew that he would never answer me again—and then realizing that I was wet from where I had peed on myself. Miss Sister was sitting right there beside the bed; as always, she was my angel, ready and waiting to take care of me. And taking care of me was what she did. I could not tell you how much time went by, but for days, at least, I could not get out of bed. There were times when Miss Sister would get in bed with me and rock me just like my mama would when I was sick as a child. During those times, I would cry uncontrollably, and the only thing that would make me stop was realizing that Miss Sister was weeping along with me. I don't know what Gabriel or our parents were doing those days, and really I didn't care. But I was sure that whereever they were, pain was ripping their hearts out just as it was ripping out mine. Miss Sister was my angel, and she nurtured me back to sanity.

Someday began to bark as I set free the river of tears caused by the pain of remembering all the disappointments I had endured. I beat against a tree, barely aware of where I was. Eventually, I moved to the other side of the tree, hoping that I would not be seen while trying with all my might to keep my voice down so no one would hear me. I was tormented enough without having to explain to anyone just what I was going through at that moment.

15

PEACE FINDS US

Spent, I rested against the tree, still crying, and realized that we had been gone for a while. Wiping my face, I said to Someday, "Boy, we need to be headed back so I can refresh myself for dinner. I should be able to finish getting this out before we get there. Now, where was I?"

Well, within a month's time, Judge Butler died from a heart attack, and a year later Mrs. Butler passed. I truly believe it was because she missed the judge so much. Before we could get over our grieving for her, my papa and mama went missing, never to be seen or heard from again. They were last seen leaving the town store and heading back home. They never arrived, and two days later, their carriage was found deep in the woods down by the river. Losing loved ones was never easy, but this proved to be even worse because there were no remains as evidence of our loss.

Despite all the tragedies, Gabriel continued on sleeping with the slave women and produced many children—but not one boy, just girls. By this time, I really did not care for him in that way, so it did not matter whether he visited my bed. When he did, though, I complied with my wifely duties. I did this until the itch came—after that I did not hesitate to ban him from intermittent occurrences. It was strange how subtly love could change to hate without anyone recognizing it until it had already happened.

Now it seemed that Gabriel and I were left alone to grow old. Gabriel became ill and remained sick for months, and as his health slowly faded, his days were filled with pain and total bed rest. Dr. Jason said it was important for someone to always be with him. Usually, I sat with him during the day, and Clem, his foot man, watched him at night, making sure that he was comfortable and that his medicine was administered on time.

Then the day came, and it was an unusual day—a day of sadness, a day of relief, and a day of fearing what the future would bring. The reality of being a widow set in. A widow still had no rights. Even after her husband was gone, all of the decisions regarding her life were now left in the hands of the next male relative. That would have been my son, but he was gone, so my fate was left in the hands of Gabriel's cousin, the son of his cousin Bunny Boaderwright-Bentley. What we did to Bunny at my engagement party seemed worth it at that time because, no matter what, every time I saw strawberries, I would laugh. I continued to laugh until years later when Bunny and her husband visited us. I truly believed that having Miss Sister whipped was Bunny's revenge for her strawberry-stained dress. Miss Sister's suffering paid for something she was innocent of. And now I was in the palm of her son's hand. Perhaps I, too, would pay for those strawberries.

On this day, my husband of so many years, Mr. Gabriel Butler, was laid to rest. Hearing those words—"ashes to ashes and dust to dust"—made it real final. Surely I cried. I wept over things—things that were good, things that should not have been, and things still to come. Only one person knew what was really hidden in my heart, and I knew my secret was safe with her.

After the burial, all sorts of people crowded the house out—people upstairs, downstairs, in all the rooms, even in the front yard, sitting on the porch, and in the backyard as well. I spoke with family, close friends, and of course those people I had probably spoken to fewer times than I could count on one hand. There were some people Gabriel had known but I hadn't, and then there were those who made me wonder if anybody knew them at all—and still I had to be polite.

The house was filled with sadness and the aroma of foods brought by the church folk and others who had wanted to share their favorite dishes—so much food that I could only hope it would all be eaten with no leftovers to be stored. But after a while, I began to realize that the crowd was dwindling away and some relatives had taken it upon themselves to take charge and make sure that the servants got everything back to order. Then the only sound was the loudness of my mind going over and over the events of the day again and again. Still, I wondered at times if this was a bad dream I would soon wake up from.

After a few days, all the out-of-town guest had left, and now Miss Sister and I found ourselves sitting on the porch. This porch seemed to be our favorite place, and with the help of the sun, it seemed to always chase the blues away.

We sat there for a while, two old ladies nodding off, until finally, she said, "Miss Margaret, you sit here, and I am goin' inside and get somebody to make us some lemonade." Since we were children, there was something so enjoyable about our drinking lemonade, so I nodded my head as she got up to go inside. She was wearing her favorite blue bonnet on her head, and I was wearing my own favorite—buttercup yellow. I couldn't help thinking about how far we had come together and how much we had survived by God's mercy and grace.

"And call upon me in the day of trouble: I will deliver thee, and thou shalt glorify me" [Psalm 50:15]. God's Word was true because He gave Miss Sister and me favor with Mark Bentley. It turns out that he was just the opposite of his mother, Bunny. This man was truly God's saint, and he made provisions for Miss Sister and me to live a comfortable life of peace and rest. Our latter days were to be better than our beginning.

Now that Gabriel was gone, things were so peaceful around the house, and often, Miss Sister and I would find ourselves just sitting on the porch, drinking lemonade and rocking while we passed the time knitting or crocheting, often at the mercy of our hands—hands that had aged so much that at times we couldn't get those old fingers to just do right.

Many days we would enjoy piddling around in the flower garden. God surely did something special when he decorated the earth with flowers; not only were they as beautiful as the colors of the rainbow, but they also made the house smell so inviting. Age united with life had worn us down, and often, we did not feel up to doing much more than just admiring the flowers. Maybe in a sweet sort of way unbeknownst to us, they brought some comfort, like a bandage that covers an ugly wound.

Now we were able to enjoy keeping each other company. Finally, we had given ourselves permission to be friends and not care about what others thought. Now we were allowed to be two old women who had weathered the storms of life. There were times when we would laugh at our memories, and sometimes, we would suddenly find ourselves staring at each other, crying as the pains of the past haunted our present as lost ghosts. But always, when those moments were over, we would sigh with the relief of being overcome with God's peace. The peace of God is so powerful that when you finally experience it, you realize that you are willing to do whatever it takes to keep it.

On one of those hot, sunny days, we were sitting on the porch, and I looked over at Miss Sister and said, "You know what?"

And she said, "What, Miss Margaret?"

"You just sit right there, Miss Sister. This time I am going to go in the house and make us a cool glass of lemonade."

We looked at each other, both thinking of how others would be shocked that this white woman was making lemonade for a slave woman, and then we smiled. I went on in the house and made us two glasses of lemonade. But the most surprising thing was that when I got back to the porch, I found Miss Sister with her head laid back on the chair, face all aglow with a sweet smile. She had silently passed on, but the smile on her face gave the impression that she had found something far better than life. My friend, the only one I ever trusted, was gone.

Miss Sister lived only seven months after Gabriel passed away. Life was so strange that way—I would have thought that after Gabriel, the one who had made her life a living hell, had passed, she would have embraced her freedom from him and lived forever and a day. But I guess being free from him gave her the peace to enter into eternal rest.

16

JUSTLY SO

After Someday and I finally reached the house, I decided to sit for a moment on the porch before going in to refresh myself. The cry had brought me much relief, and in that moment, I was so thankful for having Someday. As I stroked his back, I continued my conversation with him.

Now for me, what was left of Miss Sister were memories—and you, her dog, a dog she named Someday. I had never really thought about it before, but now I reckoned she gave you that name because she believed that someday things would be better for her. Someday, do you think that maybe if she had named you Today, it really would have happened for her?

Why, Miss Sister and I together—we shared so much. Some of those things I could talk about, but one thing in particular I dared not discuss with anybody. Now that Miss Sister was gone, my secret was laid to rest with her.

Someday was the only one I could tell it to.

You see, Gabriel had been sick for a long spell, and someone had to be with him at all times. Well, on this particular afternoon, I was taking care of Gabriel, and while he slept, I sat in the sitting room drinking a cool glass of lemonade, pondering my life, and I had a revelation—a revelation of how much Miss Sister and I had *in common*.

A white man had fathered me, and I suspected that the same man's blood ran throughout her veins. I was bound to a white man because of marriage, and she was bound to him too because of slavery. This white man was the only man I had ever been intimate with, and Lord, how I craved it so. Miss Sister shared her body with this same white man and hated it. It was my womb that gave life to his child, and her womb gave death to his child. I was not allowed to be a mother; he took my child and sent him away and kept on until he sent him to his death. If Miss Sister's child had lived, he would have taken her child and sold it into the death of slavery. I could not own anything because it was against the law for a white woman to have ownership of property. Miss Sister, being a slave, couldn't either.

Because of the pain that resided in our hearts and souls, it would have been easy for us to become spiritually dead. Why, Satan himself wanted Miss Sister and me to become enemies. While sitting there I realized that Miss Sister and I were bound together as allies for the simple fact that no one else cared to acknowledge our hell. In this, we only had each other. Mama did not want to know about it, Papa did not care about it, and the church did not care to know about it. Gabriel did not love me the way I needed to be loved, and he took all that Miss Sister would have given to the man she loved. Gabriel did all of this and felt that because he was a white man it was *justly so*. My skin was milky white and hers was not, but everything else we had *in common*, even our hatred for this white man.

Suddenly my thoughts were interrupted by Gabriel calling out for me. "Margaret! Margaret! Margaret!" Then his voice changed, his tone fearful. This fear was his wondering if I would come. I always came. Miss Sister, hearing him crying out, came rushing into the sitting room to see where I was and if I was aware of his calling me. But before she could say anything, I said, "Miss Sister, sit down and enjoy a cool class of lemonade while we allow that white man to die—and it is *justly so*."

·

Printed in the United States
By Bookmasters